This story is a work of  incidents are fictitious and any similarities to actual persons, locations, or events is coincidental. This work cannot be used to train artificial intelligence programs.

No AI tools were used in the writing of this book or to produce the artwork thereon.

ISBN: 978-1-998763-42-9

All rights reserved.

PAINTED DEAD GIRLS Copyright © Atlas Wundor 2025

Logos included in/on this volume Copyright © 2025 Unnerving

Cover photograph by Wes Hicks

PAINTED DEAD GIRLS
ATLAS WUNDOR

JULY 24, 1996

Charlaine Chabot sat up from the couch where she'd fallen asleep, hair in a busy bird's nest of wayward strands and greasy clumps. *The Daily Show* had come on and Craig Kilborn was interviewing Jon Cryer. Charlaine blinked at the man, trying to place him, then it came: he was Duckie from *Pretty in Pink*. Why he was on TV now, she had no clue. She'd caught the first episode of *The Daily Show* two nights earlier and figured it might slip neatly into her nightly rotation, at least through the summer, until school started. Come September, she'd be entering the eleventh grade, almost a senior; she'd also have to put up with a more stringent bedtime, almost a senior or not.

She reached for her glass, the dregs from a can of Diet Coke flat and syrupy at the bottom. She grimaced as the less than prime soda taste lingered in her mouth. She set the empty glass down, subtly missing perfect coverage over a white ring embedded into the table by about two millimeters. *The Daily Show* shifted to a Tampax ad, the women smiling and certain, the reason written in blue. There had been a moment between the show and the advertisement; she'd heard a creak coming from somewhere in the house. She reached for the remote, muted the TV, and sat still, listening, breath held.

Her parents had decided, last minute, to drive up to the lake to join friends, despite that it was a Wednesday. The house should've been silent, aside from any noise Charlaine made herself. Right now, Charlaine wasn't making a peep.

"Paranoid," she whispered, then added, "Probably a mouse."

The sound didn't recur, nor did any others during the following three advertisements. The show returned and Charlaine unmuted the TV to catch the rather too large applause of the studio audience. She sat back, the creaking sound all but forgotten, wondering if people got paid to sit in crowds to watch TV—how could they be relied upon if they weren't paid? Perhaps it was excitement? That actually seemed more plausible than payment; she could see herself getting pretty excited if she were at a taping of *Friends* or *Dharma & Greg*.

Kilborn made a final joke, dished out some thanks, and the credits rolled, all inside a minute. The Tampax ad reappeared, those confident women with their white, white teeth; she shut down the TV. She grabbed her glass and the bowl from a bag of microwave popcorn and headed toward the kitchen. Her mother had thrown enough fits concerning dirty dishes that it was now automatic for Charlaine to clean up after herself.

Not that her mother didn't still find things to nag her about. Lately it was how she was dressing and how long she was spending on the telephone. Charlaine never complained about it at school; tons of kids had way stricter parents. Though, sometimes at home, it seemed her parents were regular authoritarians. Once, she'd called her father a low-budget Hitler, and he'd laughed in her face. Once, she'd called her mother a bitch, and she'd slapped Charlaine in the face.

"But that's when the hornet stung me, and I had a feverish—"

Something sparkled in Charlaine's peripheral vision as she bent to load the dishwasher, silencing the earworm that had made it to her lips. Bent over, she followed the oddity and saw a small, ovular chunk of mystery material on the floor. She squinted, she reached, almost touching. Glass, but from where? Her gaze played up to the window and over the smooth pane until stopping on a hole next to the door handle.

Charlaine stood straight and said, "Hello?"

More clues tumbled into place. He was back for more, and she'd been selected.

"Nononono," she mumbled as she shuffled in her bare feet to the phone hanging on the wall next to the fridge. At the base of the phone were all the emergency numbers. Some counties, and every major city in the country, had already adopted the 911 system, but Delson had not. "Two-seven-three," she said as she punched numbers. "Five-five-nine—"

From the dim living room stepped a man in a black ski mask with yellow stripes around the brim, the word

ATLAS WUNDOR

Ski-Doo clear along both sides of his skinny head. Charlaine stared in horrific surprise, a series of steps playing through her mind.

"Huh-no," she whispered.

The man popped forward, right hand slamming the telephone's hook switch into the closed position. That stretched arm remained there, an inch from her chin as the man stared into her soul.

The seconds mounted, burying her sand in an hourglass. Charlaine couldn't move, could do nothing more than stand dumbly, her chin quivering, tears budding, gaze now locked on the scuffed and worn leather of his driving gloves; there was a hole, revealing that the nail of his middle finger had gone blue. A shiver danced through her and she peeled her attention from the hand back to the rest of the man.

"Please," she said, or perhaps only breathed the sound.

The sound seemed to end the stalemate. He took the phone receiver gently, then hung it up. He was utterly bland, unremarkable. She was 5'6"; he stood a few inches taller. Her mouth opened then closed, words now wholly defeating her. The man straightened his back, and his teeth appeared through the little mouth window of the mask. He was smiling.

"Hush," he whispered.

Charlaine looked to the counter and the knife block, the wooden rolling pin, a rusty cookie sheet standing lonely in a steel drying rack. She looked back to the man, trying to will her nerve into something akin to offense.

"Don't bother," the man whispered.

He was a man, a grown man who'd gone a lifetime aided by testosterone. He was taller. He was trim, just like her, though with obvious blue-collar muscles stiffening the sleeves of his black shirt. He had all the advantages. She needed to get to the counter, needed a weapon, needed it now.

Black gloves, black pants, black shoes. He reached behind him with both hands, As if willing her to test him. She didn't. Couldn't. She watched instead.

Suddenly, in his right hand was a knife and in his left was a loop of laces, pink and sparkly and almost certainly taken from a pair of shoes Charlaine kept in her closet, despite being old and worn.

How long had he been listening?

Had he been watching her?

Charlaine inhaled deeply, filling her lungs.

"Make a sound and you're—"

His utterly normal whisper had taken on a more frightening edge, sending the panic from her head to her legs. Charlaine spun, but not toward the counter and its implements of self-preservation, instead, she sprinted down the hall toward the bedrooms. She reached her door and was about to turn inside when a hand wrenched her shoulder, sending her to the floor hard enough that her foot came up like a dart aimed for a target. The man jerked backward as if ready to dodge a second strike. The hand with the shoelaces went to his face.

A long toenail, green polish chipped from all the edges, had poked him in the eye.

"Oh, you bitch!"

Charlaine scrambled forward, her right foot slipping and nailing the attacker in the shin. He made a sound as he bent at the knees and hips. Charlaine watched from a table position. Nature took over and she shot out her left foot, donkey kicking the man in the cheek.

He covered his face with both hands now, dropping his knife to the shag carpet. If Charlaine saw this, she disregarded it. She rolled to her knees and started running, this time to the end of the hall, her parents' bedroom, and the phone on the nightstand. She slammed the door behind her and turned the handle to engage an ineffectual lock that would act as little more than a warning. She lifted the receiver and began punching the numbers into the base, her mind awake, aware, and running. The correct digits had been seared into her grey matter.

"Delson Police Department, is this an…"

The feminine voice on the other end continued well after the door burst inward, causing Charlaine to leap, phone receiver flying from her grip. "Help!" she screamed out to the room, hoping the woman answering emergency calls might get the hint.

Any ease or subtlety disappeared from the man. He stalked forward, Charlaine's arms rising to block an attack to her face, leaving her temples exposed. She didn't see the swing, didn't react. The bulb at the base of the knife's handle struck her three times before she had a chance to fall to the floor.

Moaning, almost delirious with pain and shock, Charlaine closed her eyes and began working through a prayer to the God she'd visited nearly every Sunday since infancy. Either that God did not hear or did not care…or simply never existed at all—a thought that had been refusing to leave her as of late.

Time went by in snatches.

The man put a knee on her chest and proceeded to bludgeon her about the face and side of the head. She swatted at him, blocking almost none of the impacts. He beat her head until she was out cold. She came to, briefly, and attempted a scream. She'd been gagged quiet, pantyhose around her mouth.

"Enough," he said, voice hoarse and grunting as he punched her square in the chin.

Charlaine went out then.

The man then lifted her onto his shoulder and hurried to the back door. Outside, the siren song was clear, but didn't matter. It was already too late. He'd struck again. He'd strike for as long as it took to get things perfect; it was obvious the police would never catch him.

He broke through the rear gate of the Chabot property onto a residential alley populated by garbage bins and discarded couches, cats sitting high on the seemingly endless privacy fences. Privacy fences could be a pain, but for this step, they were like a magician's cover cloth. He rounded out to a dead-end street where he'd parked. Lights were on in some homes, but more were dim, lifeless.

Behind him, he heard police officers shouting as they entered the Chabot home. The girl they sought, of course, was gone. Now you see Charlaine Chabot, now you don't.

At least, not until he was through with her.

1

MAY 9, 1997

Jaqi Bazinet took a deep breath, attention affixed to the digital readout of the dash's clock as she rubbed a finger over a gravy stain that had refused to come out in the wash. She had ten minutes before her shift started; the perfect amount of time to commit a little self-harm.

She sighed. There was no getting around it. She glanced to the clock once more, fingers on the door handle, watching until she had only nine minutes until her shift.

With a huff, she kicked open her car door and started across the parking lot. The late afternoon sun pounded the greyed asphalt like it had a vendetta, sapping it of luster and cracking its surface. The Bell Telephone booth next to the clubhouse was clean—just out of town, it didn't get the same use as those where more traffic passed by, didn't get the bored riffraff as did the booths in town. She stepped in, the plastic scent thick enough that she could taste it. Heat enveloped her between those three walls, instantly pebbling her forehead with perspiration.

From her purse came her wallet, from her wallet came the calling card her father had provided the day he helped move her into a freshman dorm. She'd only ever used it to call him. If she did call another number with the card, he'd want to know who, what they did or wanted to do, all so he could judge them according to income or inheritable wealth. Strangest part, she didn't think he knew he was obsessed with how much money people made.

An older style phone, she couldn't swipe the calling card. She set the card in the stainless-steel frame around an advertisement for Crime Stoppers and punched the digits in as she read them. She heard a faint click that let her know she was connected, then began to punch the phone number in from heart, pausing before pressing the final six.

"Don't answer," she said beneath her breath. "Don't an—"

"Hello?"

"Hey, Dad," she said, forcing a smile to her mouth. This was a little trick she'd learned to keep him from asking why she didn't sound happy before deconstructing her life choices thus far, pointing out what would've been better choices.

She called every week. There was no choice in this; the man had set the pace to suit him. It rarely seemed he was all that interested in talking to her.

ATLAS WUNDOR

"Jaqi," he said, not a question.

Her mother had died two years ago. She'd been checking their post office box when she dropped like a stone at the feet of seven retirees checking their own boxes. The aneurysm gave no warning and took without leaving behind a crumb. Darren Bazinet had sought someone to sue, and when he couldn't force the universe to pay, he moved sideways rather than onward.

Jaqi played with the hem of her work shirt. "Yeah, Dad."

The knit picking, the snide remarks, the tightening leash, Jaqi's father had shifted it from his wife to his daughter. And just what could she say? The man paid for her education and living spaces, gave her an allowance on top, and rarely said a word about her boyfriend—a man he showed no interest in getting to know, because—Jaqi assumed anyway—he figured it wouldn't last.

"Shit sakes!" a voice shouted a moment before the hollow clunk of golf balls bouncing on asphalt filled the lot with chaos. Two men were running around, collecting the balls as their bounces shrank and spread.

"You at work?" Darren said, mild disgust in his tone.

The man did golf, sure, but he golfed with purpose. The sport was built for talking shop and developing monied relationships. Most of the wealth around Delson, Ontario came from development, but these rich had literal dirt beneath their fingernails and only wore suits to funerals and weddings. Perhaps a Christening.

Jaqi closed her eyes, forced the smile wide. "Yeah,

these guys just dropped about twenty balls, good for a laugh before my shift."

"Doesn't sound like you're laughing."

A sigh wheezed free as her ruse deflated a modicum. "Well, not laugh out loud funny."

"I see." There was a pause, then Darren said, "You called?"

He said it as if she ever had anything to tell him, as if it had been her idea to call every week but this time it was because of *news*. She doubted he even wanted to talk, it was the act he liked. Talking to a daughter every week was proof of his control, whether he acknowledged that or not.

"I was just saying hi."

"I see. I was talking to Duncan's mother the other day. He's gotten himself engaged."

Jaqi nodded, nothing surprising there. She and Duncan Gillis were an item in high school. They went to prom together, had shared a limo with six other kids, designer tags hidden along the inner seams of their glitzy getups. Duncan cried when she dumped him a week later. A week after that, he was dating a doctor's daughter who'd inherited none of her father's brains but had inherited her mother's face and curves.

"That's nice."

"Duncan's working the summer in Larry's office. He'll be set for life the moment he graduates."

Jaqi rolled her eyes. Duncan's money was old enough that the family estate in England was treated like a museum. He'd have been fine if he'd taken on a coke habit and a hooker addiction.

Big smile re-affixed. "That's so nice for him."

"Uh huh," Darren said, then after a breath said, "Mike bought a helicopter."

"Your boss?" Jaqi said, her smile slipping in surprise—though why she was surprised, she couldn't say. Mike Hamilton was a millionaire and given that her father's entire value system was built around what was in another person's budget, he'd have told Jaqi of any gaudy purchase. Once, the man had purchased front row tickets for his entire extended family to see Michael Jackson in Rio de Janeiro. He charted a jet to Rio de Janeiro, booked four massive suites, and laughed away the expense when Jackson called the rest of the tour off.

"Uh huh. He's taking lessons, his sons, too."

"Cool."

"You've met his sons?"

Jesus, squeeze us. "Yes, of course."

She'd met them. There'd been two parties. At the first party they had been timid, still high school boys finding their way, not fully realizing that most of the world would kiss their asses, not just their parents, teachers, and staff. The second time they'd been about to start university—she was seventeen then. Tim, younger by two minutes, tried to kiss her as she was stepping out of one of three washrooms on the main floor of their massive home. He'd smelled of expensive whiskey and skunky weed. Don, the elder, had flat out asked her for a blowjob, had even offered to pay for it. He'd smelled fruity, like a tween's perfume. Jaqi had laughed off both the boys at the time; later, she'd had to get a girlfriend's jacket from a closet where the brothers were tag-teaming a pretty thirty-something from the catering team. From Swedish meatballs to simple meatballs; at least she'd go home with full pockets.

"Don's single."

Jaqi shook her head in short strokes, eyes closed tight, sending beads of sweat from the tips of her bangs. "There's someone waiting for the phone, and I'd best get into the clubhouse," she said, standing alone in the hot, hot parking lot.

"Okay. Love you. Let me know if you need money."

Nodding, Jaqi said, "Yes, yes. Love you, too."

She hung up and immediately felt like she'd been emptied. Where she'd find the energy to put up with customers, she did not know, but suspected she'd have to sneak a few dozen glasses of fountain Coke.

Jaqi stepped out of the booth and let the gentle breeze and afternoon sun dry her face. She took five slow breaths, filling her lungs, then emptying her lungs, voice of a college yogi in her head: "Exhale; release all that does not serve."

She stopped just inside the clubhouse. The air-conditioning was utterly glorious.

"Almost late," said an old regular as he stood at the pro-shop counter, paying for a pack of tees.

"I'm early," Jaqi said, a little curtly. "How is that

almost late? Do you need help?"

The old man only grinned at her and shook his head twice.

She sighed; this had nothing to do with a lonely old man looking for a little human interaction.

"You're going to be late. A golf course only allows for so many good shots in a day," she said. It was something she'd heard an old guy rib a young guy with one day she was driving the beer cart out to the thirteenth hole.

The old man winked. "I already had my good shots, now I'm just putting in time 'til the Reaper catches up to me."

"Look pretty spry to me," Jaqi said, mind shifting back to her father as she stepped around the counter and down a slim hallway where her boss hid whenever he wasn't working the kitchen and pro-shop.

Back there everything reeked of fryer grease. The walls were steaky with brown smudges. All but one tile of the drop ceiling was white gone to grey. The mismatched panel had originally been in a closet, away from the elements.

"Don's single," she said in a whiny singsong beneath her breath.

Nothing was ever really good enough for her father. He could father six broad-shouldered sons and buy sixteen helicopters and, still, he'd be eyeing boys with broader shoulders and jumbo jets. As far as her father was concerned, Jaqi probably hadn't made a wise move since her mother died, the very moment he began taking an interest in her moves.

Jaqi knocked on her boss' mostly closed door.

"Yeah?" he said.

2

"I'm ready. I won't screw it up again," Nick Price said, forehead and pits sweaty, fingertips black with newspaper ink.

Marcel put up a soft palm.

"Seriously. Nobody will double check more stringently than me, going forward, I mean." Nick winced inwardly at hearing the sniveling desperation in his tone. He'd never been one of those strong men with impenetrable confidence and a knowledge that success was around any corner he chose to walk. He'd never been quite so weak sounding, either. At least not in adulthood.

"Just…go clean the coffee pot. I'll let you know when I'm sending you out again," Marcel Rogger said; Nick currently stood looking over Marcel's left shoulder at Little League baseball photos. "You're lucky we're keeping you on at all. Be thankful. Be patient, too."

"I can do small stuff?" Nick said. Cleaning was not what he'd graduated college for, was not what he'd been employed to do those seven months ago.

"This is either school or baseball, neither is *small*." There was anger in Marcel's voice.

Defeated, Nick slunk away. Three weeks prior, Nick had been given his first *real* assignment: follow up on a string of sexual assaults in the area. Prior to this, he'd covered high school plays, a dog show, three artisan fairs, took notes and recordings of town council meetings—though he never had to write those up; Marcel covered everything political himself—and more than one hundred street Q&As, which was the fluffiest kind of space filler short of using pictures of kittens or puppies. Or, in the lowest of lowbrow journalism, pictures of women in bikinis.

Now, however, he couldn't dream of getting into the pages of The Toronto Sun, unless he found he looked exceptional in a bikini. He knew he was lucky he hadn't been outright fired after the monstrous gaff he'd committed.

He'd interviewed the lead detective on the sexual assaults file, then a witness, and finally, the three victims. Two were minors, the third was a twenty-six-year-old, and in a rare show of selflessness and courage, was boisterous about her attack and publicly sought justice. Unfortunately for Nick, he misread his notes while compiling the story and ran with the name of one of the minors printed in place of the adult victim. Marcel had to print a retraction and make a public apology. Strangely, the man did not throw the new kid to the wolves, instead suggesting that every newspaper had a lot of information to double check, and that it was his job as editor to make sure what hit the printer was correct. Which was true, but how much easier was that when his journalists didn't royally screw the pooch?

Nick stood at the sink with the coffee pot and bottle of Sunlight dishwashing liquid in hands. "Reporter turned dishwasher; you're going places Mr. Price," he mumbled as he took a green scrubber pad to the inside of the pot. "Now, this is a story: newspaper employees forced to work in unsanitary conditions." The pot, which he'd thought was tinted a copper color but had gone dull over time, was in fact glass with so much old coffee caked to the inside walls that it looked, somehow, much fancier than it was. The residue came off in flakes, not unlike peeled sunburn. As soon as he saw them floating, he thought of all the times he'd seen similar flakes in his mug, had seen them until he drank them down.

Nick mock-gagged at the thought. If he didn't know the ten other employees of the Delson Mirror, this coffee pot might've been a surprise.

Behind him, Martine Cousineau waddled into the kitchen, unborn child leading the way anywhere she went. Nick smelled her perfume; it was a knock-off of something pricy, and thusly, smelled pretty nice. Which did not match her personality. She stepped to the fridge for a liter tub of mint chocolate chip ice cream she kept in the freezer. After grabbing a spoon from a drawer loaded with mismatched silverware, she flopped down onto one of the vinyl-topped dining chairs. They were 'seventies chic, brought in when Marcel remarried and his wife demanded upgrades.

"What are you doing?" Martine said from around a mouthful of ice cream.

"Atoning," Nick said.

Martine nodded as she scooped. "That fridge needs a clean, too. I can tell Marcel to tell you, or you can just do it."

Nick glanced over his shoulder. The woman looked thirteen months pregnant but was only eight. Nick had an idea that once she went away of maternity leave, he'd finally get stories again, but he'd been wrong before.

"Whatever," he said.

Martine huffed through her nose. "I'm not the one who printed the name of a sexually molested minor. If it were up to me—"

Nick rinsed the coffee pot—some edges still bore grim scum, but what the hell—and placed it on the percolator's burner. "Yeah, yeah. If it were up to you, I'd be fired."

"To start. You should be charged," Martine said, slow and oozing emphasis.

Nick licked at his teeth as he squeezed back anger. "Noted. And have you considered that not every story you write has to relate to pregnancy or kids? I mean that piece about the impending garbage strike, I'm still trying to put together the leap from trash potentially piling up and that relating to the risk of public health to pregnant women and babies. It's almost like you have the unbearable tunnel vision about seventy-five percent of your ilk come to suffer from."

Martine scrunched her bloated face. Some women glowed and some women seemed to pulsate; any glow Martine harbored was more like the shine from radioactive waste. A grin quickly replaced her angry expression.

"You think you'll get stories when I'm gone, but Marcel's already interviewing my replacement, and yours."

Heat barreled up Nick's collar. "What?"

"You're through. He's just a coward about firing people. He can't stand the awkwardness. You're a regrettable footnote in the history of the Delson Mirror."

"I'm going out for a smoke." Nick filled a glass from the tap, and stalked off, toward the back door.

At first, Martine had acted as if he didn't understand how big of a screw up it had been. Now, she steadily bashed him with it, though she'd never told him he was being replaced. That was all new and wholly troubling, though far from unexpected.

He pulled a semi-squished pack of Matinee Golds from his pocket as he shouldered open the door. The heat was something already, but not so bad right there. He inhaled deeply of the muggy afternoon air as he stepped into the shadows out back of the building, flicking his lighter and touching flame to the tip of his cigarette.

"Hey," he said as he exhaled his first drag.

Though he had assumed he'd be slipping into her role once she was gone, a part of him had been sure he was cooked. Thankfully, he'd always been a touch paranoid. He'd gone to the library six times in the last three weeks to check the national job bank on the internet. There were jobs, but he didn't feel much like uprooting and moving to one of the territories, or worse, rural Saskatchewan.

"You get that coffee pot clean?"

"Oh, god, Marcel didn't make him clean that nasty old thing?"

Outside was a picnic table and three steel Maxwell House coffee containers, rusty and overflowing with sodden, browned cigarette butts. The scent around the table was sweet, a mix of freshness and diluted tobacco smoke. At the table, Erica Bellerose and Eugene Longauer were reading newspapers and chatting their findings, cigarettes on the go, Tim Hortons cup steaming their over-hot contents.

Erica was in ad sales and Eugene covered sports and any attractions coming through the small city of Delson Ontario. Aside from Erica, there were six other advertising salespeople. The makeup of a newspaper staff had seemed curious and backward when he'd first started at the Mirror. None of his professors talked much about advertising, most simply glorified the act of purveying honest news. But that was backward. Nobody ran a news outlet to spread truth, to expose trouble, to keep politicians a tad honest now and then. News was the stuff that went between the revenue. Without advertisers, there was no paper. In fact, right around the time TVs made it into every home, the newspaper became all but redundant, shifting the ratio from 80%-20% news to ads to something closer to 70%-30%, ads to news. It did not bode well for the future.

"Clean enough," Nick said, taking a seat.

Erica shivered, as if mildly disgusted, then said, "Baby with three genetical parents born," reading from The Toronto Star.

Eugene lowered his paper, winked at Nick, then lowered it enough to look Erica's way. "How the hell they do that?"

Erica folded the paper, then plucked her smoldering cigarette from a crack between boards of the table. "Science mumbo jumbo; you read it." She looked at Nick. "They give you anything yet? Or is it more cleaning?"

Nick shook his head, exhaling a plume of grey smoke. "Nothing, either way."

Erica smiled at him. She was around fifty, tall and bulky, with a great sense of humor. After his colossal screw-up, she had pointed out that paper sales were up and that kind of thing increased ad sales, suggesting that Nick should get a raise instead of getting punished. Eugene hadn't joked, but he'd always been amicable, even sharing some of his biggest oversights and blunders—none matching the scale of what Nick had done.

"That Marcel's making you do the cleaning does not look good, Grasshopper," Eugene said, cigarette dangling loosely from his lips as he scanned the paper.

"I guess. I don't even get how everything's so dirty in there. They have cleaners, right?" Nick dragged hard, his chest filling, accepting the modicum of magic that cigarettes seemed to offer.

Erica flicked her butt toward the Maxwell House cans. "The cleaners are bona fide retards."

"Can't say that. Mentally handicapped," Eugene said, taking up The Sun and flipping through the pages.

"Yes. Sorry." Erica shook her head, not smiling now. "I have trouble keeping up. When I was a kid, we called them all Mongoloids."

"Yeah, my parents—wait, what?" Nick said, plucking a confusing bit of information from what she'd said.

"The cleaners are mentally handicapped. The government covers half their pay, so we put up with a moderately clean workplace. They don't touch dishes anymore because a couple years ago one young man got excited and dropped a mug Marcel's mentor had given him." Eugene flattened the paper on his lap and ran a finger along the tight print of the story concerning the three genetical parents. "I didn't even know genetical was a word," he said after a moment.

Nick didn't hear the final piece, his mind stuck on the fact his boss trusted him only a little bit more than the mentally handicapped cleaning crew who were subsidized by the government. Crazy. He might as well just quit; overcoming this mistake was simply too daunting, and maybe even hopeless. Of course, he had to find another job, first.

But who the hell would want him?

For a moment, Nick saw himself standing in a vast, empty field, one so flat he could see all the miles of nothingness offered by both the territories and rural Saskatchewan. He sighed, then took another deep drag which brought cinders a quarter inch from the brown paper over the filter. Done, Nick made to flick his butt toward the cans but stopped. The door swung open and Marcel, red-faced and bug-eyed, shouted, "They found Charlaine Chabot's body! Oh, and Nick, if you don't mind, clean out that fridge. Toss anything expired. Please and thank you."

Erica and Eugene leapt from the table to follow Marcel back inside. Rather than heading in to clean the fridge, Nick lit another cigarette, imagining himself throwing away a certain somebody's tub of ice cream when he did finally go back inside.

3

Jaqi jumped when a hand snaked out from under the table to beneath her skirt. Rough, sandpapery fingers pinched her ass cheek through her cotton panties. She spun to face the fat-headed goon, Randy Hyde. She'd been serving him for a month now, since her first evening on the job, but this was the first time he'd actually touched her. Prior, only his mouth had intruded on her well-being. According to Randy, she had child-bearing hips, suckable tits, and a face that would look great coated in his jizz. She'd worked twenty-one shifts and he'd come in Twenty of them. She'd begun to wonder if her boss, Chet, had handed over her schedule. Hell, he might've consulted his best customer which days and times would be best for her to come in.

"Don't you fucking touch me!" Jaqi said, hand shaking as she pointed at the big man.

"Feisty," he said, smiling, scooching himself closer, grabbing her by the hips.

His grip was disgustingly warm, and he smelled of Old Spice and concrete dust. In a blink, Jaqi imagined telling her father about this man, and his father taking action…though, in reality, her father would likely be impressed what Randy had done *and* his being only second-generation wealthy. In three generations, the Hydes might own a jet even. Something to consider.

Jaqi tried to jerk herself free; Randy gripped tighter, his fingers like dull finishing nails being driven into her soft flesh. She had been rolling silverware when Randy and his dullard sons stepped into the restaurant and sat down. She hadn't considered what she'd been doing when they'd entered, walking over with the silverware in hand. The silverware went into her apron pocket when she reached for her pad and pen and had remained there until now.

"Get your fucking hands off me!" Jaqi grabbed blindly, inadvertently selecting a fork. She reared back to stab the fork down into his neck.

"Fuck you think you're doing?"

The fork clattered to the floor as Jaqi eyed her boss who was standing in wide-eyed horror over by a wall of dusty golf cleats for sale. Chet was a big man, though unlike Randy and his sons, it was all fat. He looked as if he might load the seat of his pleated khakis.

"I…" Jaqi began, the word slipping into confused oblivion.

"Were you going to stab him with a fork?" Chet said, taking one step nearer.

Randy laughed, squeezing both her ass cheeks now as he pulled her to his crotch; his erection was obvious, straining against denim. He swayed gently in his seat, rubbing it against her. "Nah, she was only showing me how she liked—cunt!" Randy's body jerked open, right hand shooting to his left forearm where Jaqi had planted a butterknife. Blood spurted and Randy shot to his feet. "You cunt!"

Jaqi stumbled forward, face and neck red. Randy's boys were looking at her with pure admonishment, as if *how fucking dare she!* Chet stomped over to Jaqi, grabbed her by the shirt collar and threw her toward the door, which happened easily now that Randy no longer held her.

"You're fired, you fucking psycho." He turned to

Randy. "Man, I'm so sorry. Say the word and we'll detain her 'til the cops come."

Jaqi had had enough, had heard enough. Between her father, Randy, and now Chet, she needed away from men for a while, especially men in blue uniforms. She launched to her feet and broke for the exit. She heard Chet still yelling in her wake, but hardly cared as her thoughts had flipped to the bigger implications of what she had just done. Outside, in the smoggy, bird-filled air, Chet's voice had become a whine. Jaqi stumbled toward her car trying to cut through the humidity to catch a clean breath of air. Despite her body's current troubles, she was too busy envisioning the three years of university she'd finished becoming worthless, thanks to a criminal record.

By the time she got her car pointed out of the parking lot and at the highway, she was sobbing. But there was no time to gather herself. Clear both ways, she rolled out, driving on memory and instinct rather than with her eyes and mind. Something poked at her tummy; she rooted blindly around into her apron, finding a steak knife. She tossed it to the shotgun seat floor where it sank beneath a layer of plastic Diet Coke bottles, cardboard pizza triangles from takeout slices, and gum wrappers—she usually cleaned the car every couple weeks, but had been slacking since the schoolyear ended.

Once the insanity of the scene was behind her, she began to watch for cops. Every car she passed became an unmarked cruiser, maybe a detective's car, maybe something undercover—nobody would expect a cop in a

Chevy Cavalier with rust holes and a pointless hood scoop, would they? The thought of the cops kept her from going to the apartment building where she'd moved in about a month ago, though her boyfriend had been living there for about seven months now. She parked in behind the town's strip club and hurried over to the seasonal ice cream parlor across the street. She ordered two scoops of Moose Tracks in a waffle cone and sat on a weathered picnic table in the thick shade beneath a weeping willow. She licked thoughtlessly, eyes on the street, watching, waiting, knowing they'd come for her. She trailed a fingertip around a freshly carved Wu-Tang Clan emblem. Her father would suffocate her after he inevitably put money to work alongside a system that rarely punished its wealthy citizens. So, prison was unlikely…that was something.

A tear slipped down her cheek. She tried to imagine herself reacting differently and discovered a deep part of herself that was proud, wildly proud, that she'd stood up against the patriarchy. Her mother might've even been proud, then again, she might be fantasizing about a version of the woman who simply had not existed. She swiped a hand, brushing away the tear.

Almost as if she'd forgotten the thing, she took a bite from the soggy cone and the watery ice cream trapped within. When she was finished, fingers and lips sticky, she remained in place, unable to move. The only part about the scene that had been settled was that she would have to tell her father right away. A man she'd grown up calling

Uncle Paul would need to be called—Uncle Paul being Paul Horowitz, her father's longtime lawyer.

Then again, where were the cops?

If nobody came, then maybe, just maybe, she could get through this without further issue.

"Probably women stab him all the time," she whispered, fighting off the knowledge that someone being stabbed often, even now and then, was utter nonsense.

Still, she'd begun to convince herself nobody was coming to take her in. In a crash, her mind axed the idea. "Consider the fact that you aren't at home and nobody but the teenager at the till knows where you are," she said, re-balling her sticky napkin in a tight fist.

They'd come for her, were maybe even waiting at the apartment with Nick. Was there an APB out on her, her name thick as August humidity on shortwave stations? Probably. Almost certainly.

More people appeared at the ice cream parlor and its surrounding picnic tables, and she no longer felt safe, no longer felt that necessary anonymity. She tossed the crusty napkin into a big, blue barrel that acted as a garbage can and rushed across the gravel parking lot, back to her car—a car she'd purchased herself, much to her father's unimpressed amusement. She needed to know what was happening, if anything. Not knowing was so, so much worse, no matter the outcome.

4 Non Blondes were on the radio, demanding to know what was going on. Jaqi mumbled along with the hook, feeling gored. It was as if all the adrenaline she'd felt

since the incident had evaporated, taking with it her muscles, tendons, blood, and fat, leaving behind the hollow bones holding her upright.

"...*great big hill of hope, for a destination, hmm,*" she sang under her breath as she hooked a left onto her street. Kids were playing hockey, and she slowed to let the goalie in mismatched Road Warrior gear and an Easton baseball glove, stick by Koho, cart the net to the sidewalk so she could roll by.

Her mind had flipped and flopped, and she was now considering turning herself in; but what if he hadn't filed a report? No, home first. She arrived at the apartment building parking lot, spying every unusual car with curious terror. She recognized almost none of the vehicles in the lot. God, had she ever even considered them, those mysterious makes, models, years?

She parked and she watched.

"This little piggy went to market; this little piggy came to arrest me." Her chin began to quiver. She couldn't wait forever. Inside, pull the bandage, rip it free and determine treatment of the wound. "Dammit," she whispered, swiping at more tears.

After waiting in her parking spot for close to half an hour, a news report broke up the steady string of tunes. Jaqi turned up the volume, listening for her name, and when that did not come, she headed inside on shaky legs.

The hall smelled like curry, then Mexican, then curry again, then cat piss. She rode the elevator up to the third floor. At her door, she leaned in to listen. She heard voices inside, but was it the TV? She sighed. She'd come, now it was time to dive into the deep end. She jerked the door inward, following it like it had pulled her, a kite in a storm. She saw Nick sitting on the couch and the massive back of a blond-haired cop sitting in their recliner.

"There you are," the cop said once her al dente legs carried her into the thick stew of the moment.

It was too much. Jaqi stumbled backward against the refrigerator, then slipped down to the cool tile floor. As if through a fog, she heard Nick calling to her, heard the cop's deep baritone as they lifted her and laid her on the couch. The scent of freezer pizza cooking was the last point of acknowledgement before coming to at a start, her body rising stiffly as Dracula from his casket. The men were both standing above her, suggesting she hadn't been out for more than a minute, perhaps two.

"Jaqueline Bazinet?" the cop said.

"Yes?" she whispered, terrified of this new and awful future as a convicted felon. Almost worse was knowing that her father and Uncle Paul would need to know.

"My name is Pierre Allard. I'm a constable with the Delson Police Department."

"Okay?" Jaqi replied.

Nick fell in next to her on the couch, taking her hand in his. "Did you stab someone?"

"Mr. Price, if you'll allow me?" Pierre said, eyebrows nearly disappearing beneath the deep folds of his large forehead.

"Sorry," Nick said, and Jaqi squeezed his hand.

"Ms. Bazinet, you stabbed Randy Hyde with a butterknife. He wants to press charges. Can you tell me what happened?"

Jaqi kept eyes down and her tone somber as she relayed the scene in disgusting detail. Pierre listened without reaction, while Nick grew more and more angry, visibly angry: tipped brows, tight lips, revealing teeth, clenched fists, sneering mouth. The anger was impotent; if Nick wanted to get Randy in some physical sense, he'd need to use a baseball bat and would likely need to attack when Randy was asleep, and even then, he'd need a great deal of luck to stay upright against the lumberjack-like a man in the moments after a strike.

"I see." Pierre reached into his pocket and came out with a folded sheet of paper. "Nick, didn't you say you needed a smoke?"

"What?" he said, nearly shouting, head shaking in tight strokes. "What?"

"Out on the balcony. I'd like to converse with Ms. Bazinet alone," Pierre said, his gaze firm but not cold.

Nick looked to Jaqi. She nodded gently, so Nick stood, grabbed his cigarette pack and lighter from the dining table only a few feet from the sliding patio door, and stepped out. A wall of humid air wafted inside in the moments the door remained open. The building didn't have air-conditioning but was kept cool thanks to air from the sub-basement being pumped through the vents.

Jaqi looked at Nick, wondering if he felt like dealing with the bullshit of her impending court drama. Hell, they might send her to jail for a short while—Uncle Paul wasn't likely to let that happen, but it was possible she might do a wee stint, one for show.

Once he was out of earshot, Pierre unfolded the sheet of paper. "Read this aloud to me, please."

Jaqi accepted the page with shaking hands, her expression queering with confusion as she read the first few lines in her head. "Why would—"

"Just read it. Aloud. Trust me, okay?"

Jaqi sighed. She was already toast, what could reading this strange note hurt? "Given the liberties Mr. Hyde took with my personal space, I have no choice but to press charges against him. In court I will have my attorney call upon Stacy Greiss, Tanya Lamberts, Chrissy Peckham, and Melissa Connolly to give testimony regarding Mr. Hyde's rampant sexual assaults. I shall also ask my attorney to call upon Mr. Hyde's wife, Patricia, to give testimony regarding the three abortions she made public knowledge while in the presence of more than twenty local businesspersons and politicians last Christmas. I shall have my attorney call all the witnesses to testify, especially those who know the name of said minor Mr. Hyde statutorily raped and gave need for said abortion. Now, should Mr. Hyde choose to drop charges, I'm willing to forget the whole thing." She lifted her attention from the page of double-spaced type and frowned. "What?"

Pierre held up an index finger as he pulled a chunky Motorola cellphone from a holster affixed to his belt and flipped it open. He punched in a series of numbers, then put the device to his cheek. With his free hand, he took the paper back from Jaqi and held it out before him, though he wasn't really looking at it.

"Hey, Lonnie, is Dave still in? Yep, thanks." Pierre covered the mouthpiece. "All hands on deck tonight; Charlaine Chabot's body was discovered—hey, Dave, yeah, little issue. I'm here with Ms. Bazinet. Yeah, from the thing with Randy Hyde." Pierre nodded. "Sure, okay, but maybe he wants to hear Ms. Bazinet's statement first?" Pierre paused, eyes now on the page. "Well, she says it happened mostly the same as he said, and pretty well exactly how her former employer said, but she did mention her plans moving forward." A smile came to the left corner of Pierre's mouth. "Yes, I'm sure he was mad, but listen, and I quote…" Pierre read the statement aloud, and once he was through, said, "Better call Mr. Hyde back and relay that. I'll hang out here until I hear from you. Yep, bye."

"What the hell was that?" Nick said from the sliding door. The building was old, but the super down on the first floor kept everything greased and functional. Quiet.

Pierre shrugged, half-spinning from where he'd come to sit on the coffee table. "I have to say, as a former attorney, it's rare that a suspect has such a well-tuned defense from the start."

Jaqi shook her head, trying to clear the cobwebs of confusion, hands rubbing along her clammy knees—she needed a shower, she needed a drink, better yet, she needed a joint.

"What did I read?" Jaqi said.

Pierre only smirked.

"Why would a lawyer become a cop?" Nick said, frowning at the big man.

Pierre's smirk slipped away as he folded his arms across his chest. "Family reasons. I'm fairly certain I'll be fired eventually; I haven't made an arrest since I passed my probation period."

"Wait, so—" Nick began but was cut off by the ringing of Pierre's chunky cellphone.

Pierre winked at Jaqi, then flipped open the device. "Hello. Yep. Yeah. I figured." He folded the phone and pocketed it. "Mr. Hyde has withdrawn the charges, so the chief isn't going to pass the charges onto the Crown Attorney."

Jaqi put her hands to her head. Happy tears played down her cheeks. "Thank you. Thank you!" She leapt forward and latched onto the big cop.

"Wait, you said she gave a statement…what the hell did she say?" Nick said.

"Why?" Jaqi said, ignoring her boyfriend to grip another man.

"Well, I'd like to say it was for your sake, but five years ago I represented a family with a teenaged daughter. Mr. Hyde had been in an inappropriate relationship with her, though hadn't been charged because the Crown considered the evidence unconvincing. I took it to civil court. Mr. Hyde delayed, delayed, delayed, all the while he and his wife and children were smearing the girl and her family. The girl committed suicide before we could present the facts to a judge. The family, heartbroken and beaten, left town." A humor the man had harbored vanished during this explanation.

Jaqi released him and backed away.

"Can I read that? That's what she said, right?" Nick said, not in the conversation, but not forgotten.

Pierre handed over the note.

"I can't begin to thank you," Jaqi said

Nick read, expression growing more and more curious. "So, what, you're righting social wrongs? That's why you became a cop?" Nick said, still reading.

"Not quite," Pierre said, rising. He pointed a finger at Jaqi. "Again, not exactly for you, but you're welcome, and no more stabbing, please." He pulled a slim case from his pocket and withdrew a business card. "Should Mr. Hyde bother you, give me a ring. As I said, he's been known to publicly smear people who challenge him."

Jaqi accepted the card, then sank back into the couch's worn padding. Nick walked Pierre to the door, then returned, falling in alongside Jaqi.

"Holy wow," Jaqi said. She turned her head to face Nick. "I don't have a job."

Nick leaned in and wrapped his left arm around her shoulders. "I figured. I might not have one soon, too."

"That's good," Jaqi said. "Pretty sure that prick Randy Hyde owns about half the town. If you get fired, we can go someplace else."

"Yeah, but who's going to hire me? I'm about the worst, qualified candidate going."

Jaqi leaned her head against Nick's chest.

"The pizza!" Nick said and shot to his feet, breaking for the slim kitchen that separated the living space from the foyer. He pulled the slightly overcooked pizza out, then left it on the burners to cool. He rejoined Jaqi on the couch, drawing her head to his chest, resuming the mutually necessary position.

After two minutes of listening to the steady pulse of his heartbeat, Jaqi sat up straight. "We'll just have to make you more hireable. We'll have to do something big enough that printing that name comes second when people think of you."

"Such as?" Nick said.

Since money wasn't an issue, they had leeway to figure this out. She'd always worked. Her mother had put it into her head that the people around her, especially those at her private high school, had so much privilege they'd never be complete humans and that having firsthand knowledge of menial laborer was a cleanser for the soul. That meant her allowance was always more than she needed, and the excess remained in her checking account. What her father didn't know was that he was covering her boyfriend's rent, too, even before she'd moved in. Nick wouldn't have been able to cover his loan payments on top of living expenses otherwise.

"And just how do we do that?" Nick said. "How do I become hireable?"

Jaqi didn't think he was truly asking her. Her mind was elsewhere anyway: she was free, she hadn't ruined anything, and everything was going to work out. Plus, that pizza smelled pretty good.

4

The tunes were heavy and hard, but on low, the sound like road work being done just beyond The Bruce's walls—a small, homey dive bar at the north end of Delson. The brunt of the patrons, mostly men, watched the TV above the wall of liquor bottles, enrapt and quiet as they drank in something they'd all heard snatches about throughout the day.

Poor Charlaine Chabot.

They'd guessed as much, and still, in hushed, scandalizing tones, most talked circles around her inevitable outcome. None were immune to *some* gossip about the corpse.

"The main difference between Charlaine Chabot and the other girls was that Charlaine Chabot, according to the Delson Police Department, had given birth to a child no more than a month ago," said the talking head on the screen.

This was new, making the case all the more

horrifying.

"Jesus Christ, what kind of sicko..." Kris Edler said, voice trailing away, hands on an empty Moosehead beer bottle with a peeled label. He was a big man with a big, black moustache and a dense five o'clock shadow. He was currently an electrician by trade, but had been, at different points during his adult life, a police officer, a groundskeeper, a concrete laborer, and a carpenter's assistant. He was divorced with two girls who he saw every other weekend. "What kind of sicko does *that*?" he said again, this time as if expecting a reply.

"As it was with the Delson Dollmaker's other victims, Charlaine Chabot's body was discovered with a facial makeover, painted finger and toenails, doused in perfume, and wearing only a silk slip..." said the talking head as stock images and street footage filled the screen in a repeating series of snippets.

"How haven't they caught him?" Zach Soderberg said, then swigged from a bottle of Wildcat Strong. He was a handyman; jack of all trades, master of drinking away his paychecks. He had two ex-wives and three boys working on a gold crew in the Yukon.

"Real question is, is he done?" Andrei Orlov said, then tapped the bar top next to his empty glass. "May I have another?" After finding that nothing much was as it had been in his home country, Ukraine, he'd settled into a life as an unlicensed carpenter—in his former life he'd been a security guard, a veterinarian's assistant, and a butcher at a grocery store, though grew up with a cabinetmaker for a father, making his carpentry an easy step, one lacking most of the foreign differences he'd become accustomed to. Wood was wood; fasteners were fasteners.

"…from her home July, twenty-fourth, last year. The Delson Dollmaker entered through the backdoor; the method has yet to be disclosed…"

Loudly, as if battling the TV for attention, Colin Labanc—the fourth man in the row posted up at the bar—said, "Do serial killers just quit like that? I never heard of that; usually they get caught or kill themselves or something, don't they?" Colin drove a city bus, had an ex-wife out of town and no children.

The bartender, Lexy Mallette, frowning, looked to the men. There were eight patrons total. Two were playing pool, two were making out in the back corner over a round of darts, and four sat at the bar watching TV.

"Mind if I go back to the baseball game. My little sister was friends with Debbie Hutton; they found her body in February. Makes me think about how if my sister…" she trailed, shivering.

"I know what you mean. My Pauline just turned fourteen, but she looks sixteen. What if he fucking comes back, what if he shows up at my wife's house and steals my fucking daughter, what if he takes both? Makes me sick. I can't—"

"Better put on the game," Zach said. "Doubt this is the last we'll hear of the Dollmaker. Cops in this town'll never catch him. Goddamned useless tits."

Lexy took the remote and pointed it at the TV. She switched past eight stations before arriving at a game between the Mariners and the Orioles. The Mariners were up 7-1 going into the bottom of the seventh. The men didn't switch gears—nobody was really a fan of either team, though no doubt each had a preference over who might win.

"Man, they didn't find any of the bodies. It was all locals. The fucking cops are clueless," Zach said, a slight slur to his words.

"Yes," Andrei said, nodding before taking a swig from his fresh bottle.

Colin clucked his tongue against the roof of his mouth. "Them not finding the bodies is hardly anything. I mean, say someone dumps a body in your field and you don't know it, then the cops start doing random checks, you going to let them come onto your property for no reason?"

"Hell no," Kris said. "But, man, my girls. These cops...what if this sicko starts right back up? My girls, they've had dreams about him. Twice last summer they woke me up, screaming that the fucking boogeyman was in the closet. Thirteen and eleven then, and screaming about monsters in the closet. If I ever found this guy—"

"Maybe you ought to go over to your ex-wife's and reinforce some doorframes," Andrei said. "Wouldn't take much...though this man uses windows, I think."

"Windows?" Colin said. "Where'd you hear that?"

Andrei frowned, squinting. "Don't recall," he said, eventually.

The men silenced for a ten-count, then Kris slammed his palm on the bar top. "Here's what I'm saying: dude can go anywhere without being bothered; he knows where girls live and when their parents are out; he can get through doors or windows, or whatever, without making a peep; yeah, okay, scary, but he can do makeup, too. How fucking hard could a guy like that be to find? How many men know how to do makeup?"

"Morticians can, but I can't imagine Brian Raymond or Patrice Demko doing anything like that," Colin said.

Zach finished his bottle, belched, then said, "Cops won't find him. We need to watch our own neighborhoods, our own kids. Cops don't want nothing to do with a serial killer, too busy handing out speeding tickets and drunk in public fines. If it'll actually hurt someone, they won't touch it. If it'll ruin an honest, hardworking man's day, they're on it like Robert Downey Jr. on a mountain of heroin."

"You know, that's not a bad idea," Kris said. "If he comes back, I say we do what the cops won't."

Lexy leaned in closer to the men, elbows resting on a padded section of the bar's top. "Did any of you see that old German movie, *M?*" she asked.

The men only frowned in confusion, forcing her to explain the plot but not the ending. They sat enthralled, and acted as if she'd stolen something from them when she told them she couldn't recall how it ended. *M* lacked closure anyway, and would likely only piss off a group like this.

5

Was a pain in the ass that the bus didn't run past 11:00 PM in Delson. Melissa Sparks stood out front of Meyer's Mini-Putt; it was 11:21 PM. The streetlights at that end of town operated on a timer, leaving every other bulb unlit after 10:00 PM. It was warm, but the mugginess had tapered off. So often the world was suffocatingly hot after her shift ended in the air-conditioned little shack where she spent half her time elbows deep in a chest freezer full of ice cream tubs. Granted, that heat only hit when the sun was out.

Melissa had just closed the till by herself, and for only the second time. Once school let out for the year, she'd take on a junior management role. It was much more responsibility, a little more work, and hardly any additional pay, but she guessed it would look great on her college applications. The plan was to take a hospitality and tourism course, hopefully at a school not too far from home. She'd never told anyone this, but she'd always harbored fantasies of owning a roadside motel with a tiny waterpark, a curio shoppe, and maybe a batting cage or driving range simulator, even a mini putt had entered her little dream. It was embarrassingly banal.

Though she liked her job, right now, awaiting a ride from the cab she'd called moments before stepping outside, she wished she worked at a grocery store or a department store. They all closed at 9:00 PM on Friday nights. Had she been a shelf-stocker, she could've taken a bus, could've been surrounded by other employees, could've put herself in situations that felt safe. If she'd gotten out at nine o'clock, she'd already be home on the couch flipping through channels, bag of chips in her lap.

And all day people had been talking about Charlaine Chabot, as if four other girls hadn't been taken, assaulted, murdered, and dumped after last summer's kidnappings. All day her trepidation grew. Being alone anywhere felt like putting a target on a girl's back in Delson, but standing around on a dim street felt like asking for trouble.

What he'd done to those poor girls…but Charlaine was different. It was wildly horrible and yet impossibly intriguing that she'd recently given birth. One man who had come in was certain the baby had been sold, and that was likely the heart of why the man took girls. He'd suggested that raping them was probably circumstantial to the situation, or that the girls tried to barter their bodies for their chance to live on—Melissa tuned him out entirely when he started into how women used sex to get anywhere, his upper lip curling in the left corner, his eyes gone hard. According to this guy, any woman in a job that paid above minimum wage almost certainly got there on her back, legs spread. Luckily, a big man in a sleeveless flannel, dark blue slacks, and work boots crusty with old cement stepped in and said, "Only your ma did it that way," then asked for three scoops of mint chocolate chip in a waffle cone. By the time Melissa pulled the cone from the dispenser sleeve, the big mouth was gone.

It hardly relented, within five minutes she was back on the subject of the girl's body with another patron.

"Yes, I knew her."

"Terrible, yes."

"No, I can't even imagine."

Melissa had taken a single class alongside Charlaine. They were the same age, but Charlaine leaned into maths and sciences where Melissa had a knack for English, drama, art, even one woodworking credit. They'd spoken at parties, but sparingly. Charlaine's family had money; Melissa's family did not. When it came to a social dividing line in a school with about 120 kids per grade, finances were always a major point to any decision.

Now, it felt like luck that Melissa hadn't lived in Delson during grade school, or she guessed those girls going missing might have hurt her in a way running much deeper than simple fear for herself and vague sympathy for others. She saw the gaps, like noticing board games missing vital pieces, but didn't feel them the way most others did. At school, girls wailed, pounding fists against lockers while boyfriends cradled them the moment the pent frustration, fear, and uncertainty melted into sadness. Counselors had been employed, ready to chat. The entire school let out whenever there was a funeral, suddenly everyone was a dead girl's best friend. And Melissa had tried to fit in. She'd pretended tears, pretended to know the girls better than she did; sometimes not fitting in was scarier than opening your eyes in the dark and discovering someone in your house.

It certainly felt more plausible than a home intruder.

A Ford Taurus painted yellow pulled up before her, brakes squeaking. On the side was AJ's TAXI and the phone number. Melissa swung open a back door, the smoky remnants of the driver's last cigarette spilling out in a grey stream. Inside smelled enough like flowery air freshener that Melissa could taste the chemicals at the rear of her tongue.

"Thirteen-thirteen, Kincardine Street."

The driver, a little man with a rat-like face, made eye contact in the rearview and nodded. He pulled out onto the street, hooking into a U-turn so smooth it was as the road bent that way naturally. On the stereo was a talk radio station, the topic was Tony Blair and what it meant in Canada for Britain to elect a Labour Party candidate. One side suggested nothing, then the other suggested Canada was about to fall to pieces without the strong leadership of the Conservative Party over yonder. When the former demanded the latter explain, the latter attacked liberalism and Jean Chrétien. Thankfully, the ride was short. As far as she could tell, both sides were full of it and didn't much care about the citizenry, only about enriching themselves and their friends—she had her mother to thank for that tidbit; true or false, it sure sounded correct.

ATLAS WUNDOR

Melissa paid exact change to the cabbie, receiving an eyeroll that she knew was coming long before she'd unzipped her wallet. She climbed out and tossed the door closed behind her. She looked at the dark windows of her home as the cab rolled backward out of her tiny driveway. Her mother likely had to cover for someone at work—and, of course, her father had been in the wind four years now.

She flicked the carport light switch. She stepped by the minor clutter of the existence she and her mother shared and unlocked the door to the home. Inside, she flipped more light switches as she went, then doubled back to the kitchen to check for a plate in the fridge. If her mother had had the time to do so, she would've fixed her something.

No plate, she switched meal plans and grabbed a box of Ritz Crackers from the cupboard and the D'Angelo apple juice carton from the fridge. It beat the hell out of making something, and as a bonus, there were no dishes to be washed later.

"You're being lazy; eat something with substance," Melissa said in a whiny singsong, imitating what her mother would say if she was there now.

On the couch, she flipped through stations, munching from the box and sipping from the carton. Too tired to care about what basic cable had to offer, the crackers went back into the cupboard. She chugged down the dregs of the juice and took the carton to the door that opened onto the garage. She balled the carton, then tossed it toward the cardboard recycling bin. Only when she was fully back inside did she notice a smoky scent.

She wrinkled her nose. It was fire smoke rather than cigarette. She checked out each window, looking for the telltale dance of firelight coming from another home. The neighborhood appeared all but dead beneath the yellowy streetlights and pale shine banked by a half-moon riding high in the mat of night.

Melissa yawned. Probably someone was having a bonfire somewhere just beyond her sightline.

After a stop in the bathroom where she stripped down to her underwear and bra, she entered her bedroom. Pictures of JTT, pictures of The Backstreet Boys, pictures of The Spice Girls, pictures of Sawa, pictures of Leo, pictures of her friends, all of which were crudely cut and mashed into a huge, meaningless collage. She slipped out of her underwear and into a pair of dirty pajama shorts from the corner of her bed. She smelled the scent again, then inhaled deeply, the various perfumy hues of her bedroom replacing the smoke. Bra unlatched, she hung it by a strap over the skinny desk chair she'd had in all three of her bedrooms—all three that she recalled ever having. She studied her image in the mirror a moment, leaning her chest close to attack a whitehead that had risen deep in her cleavage. She wiped residue on her shorts, then grabbed the dirty t-shirt she'd worn to bed all week.

Lights out, she shuffled through the dark to climb into bed, yawning as she moved. She closed her eyes, attempting to shutdown her mind. She kept thinking of the smoke, could even smell it again. It maybe wasn't fire smoke, at least not wholly. She smelled diesel exhaust as well, though only faintly. She rolled over and opened her eyes. She could see shine banking off the hallway floor, trailing through her open door.

Long blinks muffled the light until she blinked her eyes wide and the light was gone altogether. Something about the change brought her away from sleep. For two minutes she tried to understand, eventually sitting up and reaching for the lamp on the bedside table. She squinted against the brightness. Her door had been all but closed—standing next to it, dressed in black, black ski-mask over his face, was a man. He held a knife that caught the light and glinted the blade's promise. Sticking out from a pants pocket were the stringy ends of several automotive zip ties—they made her think of weed tufts sprouting from and otherwise smooth plain of grass.

"Scream and I'll kill you," the man said, his voice low.

Melissa inhaled deeply, but before she could cry for help, the man had his knife to her throat. She stared down at the arm against her chest, above, the blade pressing a stinging edge against her soft, soft flesh.

"Roll over and put your hands behind your back. There's no reason I should kill you here. No reason."

Melissa felt the knife's departure from her throat, and she slowly rolled over, wrists and forearms flat against her back. She would cooperate. This was something, but it wasn't what happened to those other girls. She wasn't even from Delson; this couldn't be him, couldn't be the Dollmaker.

The plastic ties tightened against her wrists with a zippery report. Bound. She was being bound…just as Charlaine Chabot had been bound just like the other girls…there names escaped her…Charlaine Chabot's body was found…the other girls—Patricia, Susan, Christine, Emma—their bodies were found too. This *was* him! She was being taken!

Melissa inhaled deeply. "He's here! Help! Hel—"

She got out not another syllable after the man's heavy fist slammed into her head with nine lightning strikes.

6

Nick glanced at Jaqi as the coiffed head talking news on the screen finished up the day's top story. The channel was out of Guelph—a city with about nine times the population of Delson—and was the first time they'd seen a Delson story take the lead spot. Granted, neither had been there all that long. And, of course, the story was Charlaine Chabot, or rather, the discovery of her body.

Jaqi had been almost manic since Pierre's departure. Once things really began to settle in for her, she started to understand what had actually happened and what Pierre Allard had done for her. She'd been so low, and then so high and was now thrumming with a peculiar energy, one begging for an outlet. They'd watched TV, drank a couple beers, ate cold pizza, and went out for cigarettes—Jaqi was a when in Rome kind of smoker. All the while Jaqi had moved steadily from the kitchen to the bathroom to the couch, back to the kitchen, back to the couch, back to the kitchen, the bathroom, the couch. It was as if everywhere was too hot to stay in one place.

Nick had asked her a handful of questions throughout her paces, including what exactly she'd meant about making him more hireable. "Do you really think extending my education—and debt load—is going to do much?" he'd said, and Jaqi only shrugged, but the news report was helping to move puzzle pieces around in her head.

"Just awful," Nick said as a commercial for Molson Canadian began.

"He sexually assaulted them...she had a child, likely his child. That's something. That's a story I think anyone would read. I guess he's gotten what he wanted, huh?"

Nick turned to face his girlfriend of two years dead on. "He's a monster."

Jaqi made a finger gun and took a shot at Nick. "Yeah, and we're going to build the story together. The whole story. And we're going to craft it into a consumable meal that you can sell." Jaqi's cheeks were flushed and her eyes were wide and wet. "Papers will fight to get it if you do it right. Big places, maybe a magazine."

"What?" Nick straightened. "I thought you were going to say I should take a course."

Jaqi popped to her feet and began pacing in front of the TV. "You can do it. You have time, I mean, did you get any assignments for the weekend?"

Nick huffed. "The mold coating the drawers and vents of the work fridge...uck. There were chunks of grey stuff not even science could identify. I spent the afternoon daydreaming about burning the place down." He rubbed his hands together, shivering a little. "I can still feel the gooey grime."

"So, no?"

"Nothing. I'm a cleaner, not a reporter...apparently."

"That's what I thought. But you do have access to anything they have at the Mirror, and you have a press pass, which means you can interview people without seeming suspicious."

Leaned back, Nick folded his arms over his chest. "How are we—"

"I think we also might have a friend in the police department, don't you think?" she said, giving a nod to the door, despite that the cop had departed three hours ago. "Maybe he'll share some of the case stuff. He seems highly irregular."

"You think?" Nick said.

"I think you'll hit it...with my help."

"Hmm. That's a pretty decent idea."

Jaqi smiled. Instantly a heroic daydream flashed on the forefront of her mind: Nick and her standing behind a podium, him receiving some journalism award. There'd be reporters reporting about *him*. There'd be lights and cameras and handshakes and a job just about anywhere he wanted. Maybe he'd prove his writing chops, maybe take the story all the way to the Pulitzer. This crashed the dream because she couldn't imagine what a Pulitzer award even looked like—was it a trophy, a medal, just a piece of paper?

"Almost seems lucky I'm getting canned," Nick said.

"Me too."

After the sweet-smelling smoke dissipated, he'd slip right into a spot at The London Free Press, staying for two years so Jaqi could finish her degree, then the pair of them would move to Toronto or Vancouver, maybe he'd get on TV, be a correspondent for CBC... The possibilities were starting to excite her, the feeling mingling with all that had gone on already today.

Jaqi stopped pacing. She was still in her uniform: tight golf t-shirt, short black skirt, ankle socks. Her nose wrinkled at the fryer scent emanating from her person. As she thought of the shower, a bigger, more outlandish possibility struck her.

"What?" Nick said, looking at Jaqi's wide eyes and surprised expression.

"What if we can figure out who he is? He has to be local, right? He knows where the girls live and when they're home, home alone. Has to be someone with access—we need to put a big map right here." She mimed a box about the size of a typical picture window, pointing it at a nearly bare wall above the chintzy exercise bike they both used rather infrequently, despite that they'd moved it into three different apartments over three years. "We can look with an outsider prospective! The cops are locals, mostly, and they think they know some people. Imagine how many plausible suspects are immediately written off because they're on a detective's softball team? Or coached the chief's kid's hockey team?"

"Or was the editor of a small newspaper that really stuck it to them, even when they botched a case?" Nick said, frowning. "A map, huh? Kind of mess up the drywall with all those thumbtacks."

"Cops always use maps in movies, likely because cops in real life have to use maps, right?" Jaqi said, almost bouncing with excitement.

"Okay. We can get a map printed at the library, I'm sure. Maybe not quite as big as what you waved out there, but we can get a map. What else?"

Jaqi resumed pacing, her skirt flaring with each turn. "Once we have the map, and have everything marked out…what about interviewing neighbors?"

"Cops probably did that, maybe we can see the files?" Nick said. "Talking to the general public is about as fun as it sounds…most times. Granted, once they realize you aren't there to sell them anything, they tend to open up more."

Jaqi nodded. "See! We can do this. Better if you got

all fresh stuff anyway. If we get help from that cop, I doubt it'll be anything you can print. You can ask who was around, if anything's suspicious, even if they had vibes or something. Really try to paint a picture of Delson in the midst of this thing. Maybe if you teach me how to do it, I can be like your interview assistant; you know, get everywhere you can't?"

Nick fell into slow nods, his eyes gazing vacantly through the patio door.

"We can do this."

"I wonder who he is," Nick said, musing. "No doubt it's a man. Sexual assaults, semen residue, Charlaine Chabot's pregnancy, that's a man."

"What if it's not just one guy? What if it's a team?" Jaqi clapped her hands together in a single, echoing smack. "Maybe even with a woman involved. That might explain the makeup."

"Okay. But at least one man for sure."

Jaqi stepped to the TV and put her hand on the warm, black plastic. "We should watch some movies about tracking killers, figure out what kind of questions we need to ask." Jaqi looked at the clock. "What time's Blockbuster close?"

Nick looked at the clock then, too. "In like nine minutes."

Jaqi sighed, crossed the small space, and dropped back onto the couch. "Shit." She rubbed at the top of her bare thighs, then stopped abruptly. "I smell like French fries. I need a shower." She popped to her feet.

"Right," Nick said, rising. "I'm going to grab a beer and a smoke."

"Or..." Jaqi said. Her body knew how to release all that pent energy, and it was all the better if Nick gave her a hand, and maybe a little more than that on top.

Nick's eyebrows shot up. "Or?"

"Or," Jaqi said, nodding to the bathroom.

"Or," Nick said, nodding now as well.

Jaqi started toward the bathroom, Nick following her, stripping away his shirt as he walked. The space was small. Jaqi bent to reach for the tap. The flow splashed. She pulled the plunger to engage the showerhead. From behind, Nick's hand snaked up her skirt and squeezed the cool flesh in a way not so different to what Randy Hyde had done, yet infinitely different. She pressed back against the touch.

7

Cold bottle of Wildcat Strong weeping in his grasp, Zach knelt next to a cruddy Honda lawnmower he'd purchased during better times. He inhaled deeply as he steadied his stance, taking in the fresh cut grass scent—far and away the best part of any landscaping gig he'd ever picked up. He had a matching weed-whacker to go along, had scored the latter at half-price since he was buying a mower, too. It had been a relatively small investment that generated instant capital. A large percentage of Delson's population did not like to mow their lawns.

As long as he minded the oil and the blades now and then, the engines always started without argument. Cold, hot, wet, sandpaper dry, if you asked Zach Soderberg, Honda made the best lawn care tools. If he came into some money—and he managed not to drink it all—he thought he'd buy a Honda riding mower, shift fully from handyman to groundskeeper during the summer months. Being outside and riding level beat the hell out of crawling around beneath machinery, in sewage pits, boiling on rooftops, being arm deep in an old woman's toilet. If he had lotto winning money, he guessed he'd abandon it all and buy a farm, maybe buy a wife from some Asian village or Russian backwater or wherever mail-order brides came from.

"One thing at a time," he said as he dropped backward into a lawn chair, the ribbons frayed and strained to the brink of tearing. His knees were singing whenever he crouched too long as of late. He tried to avoid thinking about doing what he did for a living at age sixty.

He tipped the beer to his lips and let the cool, stiff contents fizzle down his throat. Already this morning he'd checked the oil levels in the Hondas and sharpened the chains of his matching Stihl chainsaws—he'd learned to keep two; one inevitably harbored an attitude the moment it was time to put hard hours in. True summer was more than a month away, but today felt like a preview of the heat to come.

"Not getting any cooler," Zach said, trying to psych himself into motion.

The chair felt good.

The beer felt better.

He remained sitting in his cluttered garage. The house was on a private acre of land at the south end of Delson, not far from the dump and the water treatment plant, where on bad days, when the wind blew just wrong, his house smelled like trash and human waste. His father had bought the house back when the dump was a fledgling heap of discards and the water treatment plant was over by the river. The man had paid $2,600 in 1964 for the land, which had water, electricity, and sewage access at the ready. If it was possible, Zach would've sold off more of the land, but the house was set back on the lot, making an acre as small as it could be severed without moving the house.

From the rolled sleeve of his t-shirt Zach produced a battered John Player's cigarette tin. He lit an unmarked dart—not Player's brand at all, he bought them by the bag from the Six-Nations Reservation about an hour southeast. He could score eight cartons' worth of cigarettes for the price of a single, regularly-taxed carton.

After a drag, he pounded down the final third of beer from the bottle on the go, burped, then slipped the empty into a 24-box on the floor with fifteen of its brethren, all without rising from his seat.

"No delaying it now," he said, sighing, knowing if he delayed, he'd crack another brew, then another, and another, and so on. "Up we go." He stood, remaining still long enough for his head to adjust to the change.

He took the mower's handle, tipped the machine up on its front wheels, then let it drop down, knocking two big, moldy clumps of grass onto his garage floor. Cleanup came at the end of the day, always…well, sometimes it happened first thing the following day. He pushed the mower to the edge of the garage, leaving him in the shade and putting the machine beneath the pounding sun, and gripped the recoil rope's handle. A moment before he could pull, a Ford Ranger turned onto his lane.

"Huh?" he said, hands leaving the mower.

Kris Soderberg's Ranger parked behind Zach's F-150. "Heya," he said as he climbed out of the truck.

"Want a beer?" Zach said, work forgotten.

"Sure."

"What's up?" Zach said, back to his friend as he went to the pill-shaped Maytag fridge almost twice his age to grab a couple bottles.

"Last night, remember what Lexy was telling—"

Zach handed off a cold bottle, grin playing the left side of his mouth up. "You convince her to go home with you?"

Kris snorted. "I wish. Last girl I convinced to come to my place was Wilma Kastanov."

"Me too!" Zach said, howling laughter.

Kris shook his head gently. "Pretty sure we've all had

Wilma."

"Maybe not Andrei. Never heard of him riding a moped or a butterface."

Kris shrugged. "Who knows what he gets up to? Anyway, I asked Lexy about the movie she was talking about. She used to date that librarian who was here a few years back, remember that guy?"

"The long-haired guy?"

Kris nodded. "Yeah."

"Okay."

"Anyway, he built up the library's collection of videos. All these weird, foreign movies. She was telling us about this movie and these mobsters started up like a neighborhood watch with all the bums and cornered this pedo' in a warehouse, I guess—"

"I was there still," Zach said.

Kris blinked, shaking away the confusion. "Right, sorry, but I was thinking, you and me, we should start a kind of watch."

"Movies?"

Kris scrunched his face. "What? No. Neighborhood watch."

Zach tilted his head, nodding slowly, his expression souring into genuine anger. "Yeah?"

"Sure."

Zach went back to the fridge for more beer before leading the way into the home. "Don't mind the mess." He held open the door with his right hand, which now held two beer bottles by the neck. As Kris passed him by, he said, "What if he never comes back?"

"All the better, I guess. Delson'll be safer...but I have a feeling he ain't done."

Zach stood at the door an extra moment, looking at the lawnmower. This would likely put him behind all week. However, if there was one sort of task that could be skipped over others, it was working around the yard. Nobody paid when you cut your own lawn.

Zach pulled the door closed. "If he ain't done, he's in for a world of hurt."

8

Jaqi arose early. Since she'd showered last night, all she needed to do to face the world this morning was tie her hair into a manageable ponytail. She stepped into the kitchen, looked at the clock, then looked at the coffeemaker.

Nick wouldn't be up for more than an hour. The jitteriness from yesterday hadn't fully left her system. She grabbed her keys, slipped her feet into a pair of foam and leather sandals, and headed down to her car.

She drove with the driver's window down, basking in the cool morning and the pale sky above. Stopped at a light, her nose fixed a target for her expedition. Did anything smell better than McDonald's? The taste never, ever lived up to it, but that specific fryer scent made promises strong enough to blank one's of just how mediocre the food really was.

The drive-thru was vacant as she pulled up to the talk box. The voice on the opposite end sounded sleepy and very young. Jaqi ordered an egg and bacon McMuffin meal, large coffee on the side with a delightfully crispy hashbrown. She parked with her nose pointed at a brown garbage can with about twenty white splotches of gull shit accenting the molded body.

Finished eating, she sipped from her cup, thinking about the story, the girls, and what it might mean for Nick to get it right. Down to the dregs, she finished her coffee and bagged up her trash. As she got out, an old man was headed in her direction. He had a newspaper rolled in his hand, a slightly bigger bag of garbage pinched between two fingers.

It was the Guelph paper, a city more than an hour south, but Delson had made the front page—below the fold. BODY RECOVERED was in huge black lettering, just below, in print larger than the typical font, though smaller than the headline was: Charlaine Chabot, from teen to kidnappee to mother to murder victim; what's being done?

"Are you through with the paper?" Jaqi said.

The man smiled at her and held the paper and his trash out at her. She instinctively grabbed both.

The man laughed. "Didn't need to take my garbage,

too."

Jaqi blushed. "An exchange, for the paper."

Both bags went into the garbage can, and the paper remained under her arm as she stepped back to her car.

She opened the paper over the steering wheel and stared into the pretty blue eyes of Charlaine Chabot from the past year's school photo.

Last summer, this beautiful girl had her life stolen.

Jaqi reread the first line of the column, feeling her gaze go fuzzy with tears. This wasn't a TV character or somebody in an unimaginable Third-World village, this was a girl who looked a lot like Jaqi had at fourteen, fifteen, sixteen, seventeen, and she lived in the very town Jaqi now resided. It was the ultimate unluckiness that out of all the normal, hectic, emotional lives of teenagers, this one had to be stolen.

A tear slipped, splashing onto Charlaine Chabot's face. Jaqi closed her eyes tight for a five count. When she opened them, she saw a skewed version of herself, something like what Jaqi's daughter might look like in her teens—should Jaqi ever have a daughter. Her heart began to pound, and the lovely McDonald's scent festered like a chunk of rotten meat lodged in her sinus. She spun the key, jerked into reverse, and peeled out of the lot, knowing following this story was much bigger than just making her boyfriend employable.

She burned it through town and back to the apartment, ignoring the way one of her back tires jutted over the line of her parking space. She broke for the building like she had to pee. Thankfully, after the impossibly slow elevator—an elevator that had felt impossibly fast yesterday—reached her floor, she burst into through the apartment door to find Nick awake, though still wearing only boxer shorts.

"What're we doing again?" Nick said. He was stretched out on the couch with a bowl of Frosted Flakes, an old Felix the Cat cartoon on the TV.

Jaqi had to run with the half-truth; the complete truth felt too complex for words alone. "We're making you hireable! Come on, we can't get lazy about this or you'll end up working some factory job that sucks, you'll get fat and go bald from hating your life, I'll get so disgusted by your presence that I'll cheat on you, you'll find out, we'll break up, and all because you wanted to watch dumb cartoons instead of working on this story."

Nick smiled. "You have some imagination, my dear."

"Move, bitch!" Jaqi grabbed the flyswatter from a pocket hanging at the side of the coffee table and began to thrash her boyfriend over his boney shoulders and skinny arms. "There's no time to sit around!"

Nick squirmed and squealed, finally accepting his fate and rose from the couch. "Enough. I'm moving."

Jaqi left him be to bus his bowl to the sink and hurried off to their bedroom to get dressed. She closed her eyes and thought of the amalgamation of herself and Charlaine Chabot. It was impossible that they could move quickly enough on this story.

—

As he stepped into a thrice-worn pair of Levi's, he wondered if he'd still have a job by the end of next week. In the medium run, it might be easier that way; he and Jaqi could head back to London, and he could work wherever, maybe do some freelancing to keep his toes in the correct pool. In Delson, he'd get nothing. The general population knew of him, knew what had happened, and almost certainly put him into one group or another, neither likely to be all that employable.

No, leaving, freelancing, being anonymous, that was the way forward. Hell, it was possible that thoroughly covering this story could work. Even at half as well as he hoped, he might swing a position entirely in his field. Maybe even somewhere big enough that he wouldn't need to rely on Jaqi's father covering the rent.

Getting around to that way of thinking hadn't been immediate, so Nick let Jaqi plan their day. She'd been thinking about this in a way he hadn't. Last night it sounded like something that might work, it also sounded like something that might fizzle away with a good night's sleep.

They took Jaqi's car. Whenever possible they left Nick's clanking rust bucket parked, it had been mostly reliable so far but felt as if it might shake apart at any future pothole or speedbump. Nick rode shotgun with his arm dangling out the window, occasionally tapping the steel of the door's outer panel or making his hand into a fin, let it ride a wave, mind half there, at best.

When he'd first moved to the small city, Delson felt

like a village. It took only a few minutes to get from one end to the other—took maybe fifteen minutes on weekdays as shifts at a furniture and casket factory let out only minutes after bells rang at the elementary, secondary, and high schools. Still, upon first impression, if he was the one dictating whether a city was called a city, Delson wouldn't have made the cut. According to the signs at three of the four routes in and out, 30,000 people lived there. The fourth option led directly into farmland and someone had decided to spare some expenses and put up a plain sign reading only DELSON.

It took a while to settle the fact, but Nick decided Delson was a city. There were homeless people, a methadone clinic, four ice surfaces at the arena—plenty to house the minor hockey teams, a Junior C team, and a Senior B team—a McDonald's, a Burger King, a Harvey's, four different department stores, five groceries, and more cops per citizen than anywhere he'd ever been. Of course, they were wildly easy to find—at any given moment, there was a good chance a cruiser was parked in Tim Hortons, officers sitting inside at tables in the non-smoking section. Eventually he learned that Delson even had a few whores, not that he'd needed their services. The homeless, the junkies, and the whores, those three felt decidedly citified. Especially when they ran in groups, as small as they might be.

Jaqi, squinting against the sunlight pouring in just below the visor, singing along to Roch Voisine on the radio, pulled into the library parking lot, which sat near the top of a tall hill to the north of the shopping district. The library itself was a three-story redbrick building with a green roof and wrought iron handrails and accents everywhere necessary. The windows were smoky glass. The lot itself was gravel. A folding sign by the entry stated there was a Weight Watchers meeting starting at 11:30 AM.

"Well," Nick said, reaching to tug the door handle.

"Well," Jaqi said back as she zipped up her purse.

Nick opened his door and stepped out. He stretched his back, eyes closed to the brightness of the morning.

"Warm one already," an old man said.

Nick nearly jumped, having failed to notice the man when they'd pulled in and parked. The old man was sitting on a decorative boulder next to a small tree and a strip of grass, glossy wooden pipe between his boxy teeth, stainless-steel thermos by his feet.

"Sure is," Nick said, quickly regaining himself.

The old man pulled a tobacco pouch from a pocket of his loose trousers. "Hear they found Charlaine Chabot's body?"

"Terrible," Nick said. "Just awful." It was easiest to agree on certain subjects, kept him from getting into wholly speculative conversations.

Jaqi climbed out and started across the parking lot, was already a few steps ahead, when she slowed and looked Nick's way, though didn't stop.

Nick himself had been inching away from the old man, certain inane conversation was seconds away.

The man fingered tobacco into the pipe's bowl. "You know, they ain't the first girls murdered here. Back in 'eighty-two, then in 'eighty-three, those were the first."

Nick stopped inching and turned fully around to again face the man. He called out to Jaqi, "Hey, hold up a second."

Jaqi was almost to the entrance, her brows furrowed now. It gave Nick a minor thrill to change her plans a bit; she was the type to set an itinerary and stick to it. He never mentioned it, but her father was the same way, always trying to wrangle life into a steadfast path.

"Two girls the first year and three more the second. Three different men are serving time, and I don't doubt it a bit that the same sick sonofabitch who killed Charlaine Chabot did them all. Two are perverts they got on other charges on top of murder, so I don't care about them. But one of them is a retard. They told him soon as he admitted to killing the girl, he'd get to go home."

"The cops?" Nick said, halving the space between them in a single step. He opened his messenger bag and rooted around for his tape recorder.

"Rube, Rube the Tractor Tube. That's what we used to call him. He's the chief now because he got those men locked up and quieted the killings," the old man said, then put his pipe between his teeth, wiped his right palm on his pants, and finally held out his hand in greeting. "Sylvain Beaupre."

Nick shook the offered hand. "Nick Price. I actually work—"

"I know who you are. That Marcel Rogger is smooth. I'm surprised you weren't sued."

Nick flushed. "Yeah, I screwed that one."

Jaqi came to stand next to Nick. "Hello," she said, winning smile on full display.

Sylvain pointed a gnarled finger at Jaqi, eyes going wide, expression excited. "You stabbed that meathead, Randy Hyde, right?"

It was Jaqi's turn to flush. "In self-defence," she said, sheepishly.

"Don't doubt it a second." Sylvain said from around the pipe's stem as he swiped a match against his bristly cheek, then dropped the lit end into the bowl. He took two puffing breaths and let the smoke billow away. "You here for books or a story, Nick?

To say he was or not didn't matter; he already had his recorder out. "I'm always open to hearing a story. I guess you were around when those other girls died; was it similar to what happened last summer?"

Jaqi looked at Nick in surprise.

The man repositioned the pipe stem without using his hands, letting it settle in the right corner of his mouth. "That's right, miss, Delson's not new to dead girls."

—

Two officers sat at desks in the station's endlessly smoky bullpen. Light shined in through the heavy, yellowed drapes, banking of a sea of floating dust particles. The officers were only feet apart, between them were two messy cubicles that belonged to guys on other shifts.

One of the officers in the office then was fixing paperwork, the other was reading the Toronto Star. Both had empty coffee mugs next to their typewriters. It was quiet but for the steady hum of ceiling fans and the clunky fridge in the breakroom.

"Anything interesting?"

From behind the paper came, "Looks like they arrested that DeLorean guy—"

The door into the bullpen flung open hard enough to bo oing the stopper like a physical comedian's fallback plan, disrupting the newborn conversation. Robert Thompson held the door open, and Donny Tiffany hurried in ahead of the officer. Robert, Rube, came waddling in on his tail, letting the door wheeze shut on its greasy, failing piston. Donny was a tall, frumpy man with a meaty gut and big arms; he was thirty-four. Even to someone who didn't know him, it would be obvious that the guy had more mental obstacles than the average. He was scanning the space with wide-eyed surprise, as if he'd always wondered what the police station looked like beyond the intake desk. Robert led the cuffed man into one of their two interrogation rooms—the flesh around the shiny steel was bulging, red, fatty.

This occurred at 4:39 PM.

They stepped into an interrogation room, and by the time the door closed, the officers in the bullpen were back to discussing John DeLorean and the sting that trapped him.

"Are you thirsty?" Robert said, playing nice.

"Maybe," Donny said, then added, "Are they talking about those cars? I saw one, once. Came right down the street. I was in Peggy's. She gives me ice cream cones to sweep the sidewalk out front. I ain't seent one a those since."

Robert nodded as he hit RECORD on the bulky machine made up of a cassette deck and single speaker, foldaway handle currently folded away. Outside, the mob of reporters had increased significantly since the chief was forced to step down two weeks ago. He'd put away a man for the first two murders, and this third was all but identical, suggesting that he was the kind of man to lock up an innocent man—innocent of those murders, anyway.

"Donny, what do you know about the missing and murdered girls?" Robert said.

"Oh, that's bad. Mom won't even have it on in the house," Donny said, eyes bugged, serious. "But they talk about it on the loading dock. Ricky and Terry know all about it. I work down there two days a week. I cain't do any of the machine driving, but I get to watch. Other day they had to use a crane to—"

"Can you tell me about them?"

"About the crane? Only one cra—"

"No. The murdered girls."

Donny slumped some, frowning. "Mom don't like me talking 'bout that stuff...can I have some pop?"

Robert nodded again, smiling, being so, so friendly. "Soon. Tell me about the murders."

Donny frowned deeper. "They were sexed

before…Ricky said he would have sexed all them. Mom don't like no S-E-X talk neither."

"Do you think about sexing girls?" Robert said.

Donny flushed. "Mom says that's personal, locked behind doors. S-E-X, that's between man and his wife."

"But you wonder about sex and pretty girls, don't you?" Robert kept nodding. "Those pretty girls made you excited, so you got to know the case, yeah? You learned how that bad man did it?"

Donny nodded along. "Okay."

"That's a yes or no question, Donny," Robert said, still nodding.

"Yes," Donny said, almost mesmerized.

"So, you learned what Brian Ramage did and did it yourself?" Robert said, nodding faster.

Donny matched pace. "Learned? I…I ain't very good…I didn't get to go to school long as everybody else. But I sweep good and if nobody distracts me I can—"

Robert quit nodding and stopped the tape. "I'll go find you some pop, be back in no time." He stood, leaving Donny, locking the door behind him.

It was 7:57 PM the next time Robert entered the room. Donny had been calling out and knocking on the door for more than two hours now.

"Whoa, whoa, what's with the excitement?" Robert said, polystyrene cup half full of flat Pepsi. "I was only gone a minute or two, wasn't I?"

Donny shook all over, drinking down the soda in a single draught. It was clear he'd been crying: his cheeks streaked, his flesh puffy. "I wanna go home," he said, a deep whine in the words. "Mom's gonna be angry."

"You will, we just need to go over something. After studying what Brian Ramage did to those pretty girls, you decided you wanted to try it yourself? You wanted sex?"

Donny's chin quivered. "Don't tell my mom. She's gonna be so mad at me for talking 'bout that. I need to go home."

"Do you watch them?" Robert lifted his left eyebrow high. "Did you watch them and go home at night and play with yourself."

Donny flushed. "I wanna go now."

"Soon."

"Please. I'm a get in trouble with Mom."

"You'll be out of here in no time. Just tell me again." Robert hit RECORD on the machine. "Kendra Walker, you saw her and thought she was sexy, right?" He began nodding again.

"I wanna go home." The words rode a blubbery sob from his dry mouth.

"You will." Robert continued nodding. "Just tell me that you took Kendra Walker."

"I took her. I—"

"Yes, I know. This is hard, but it will be over soon." Nodding, nodding, nodding. "After you sexually assaulted her, you put a knife in her throat, yes?"

"I wanna go home," Donny said, moaning, wailing, breaking down.

"You will, once you answer all my questions, okay?"

Robert's nodding became more emphatic.

"Yes."

"Can you say that again?"

"Yes!"

"One more time."

"Yes! Yes! I wanna—"

"Did you sexually assault Kendra Walker, then murder her?"

"Yes! Mom's gonna be so mad at me."

Robert's nodding ceased, a smile slicing his chins and lower lip from the rest of his face. "Ten more minutes and you'll be out of here."

Robert stood.

"No! I wanna go hooo-oome!" Donny launched to his feet, bringing his big hands up to grip Robert by the collar. Mentally he was weak, but physically, he was strong. Much stronger than the officer.

Nightstick in hand, Robert thumped Donny until he was nothing more than a cowering puddle of tears, blood, and slobber in the corner of the small room. On his way out, Robert gathered up the bulky recorder.

At 12:31 AM, Robert re-entered the little room. Donny was asleep, his face lumpy and purple. A green knot bulged from his forehead. He snored a sawmill of sounds, his fat belly rising and falling cartoonishly.

"Time to go. You just have to sign your name." Robert pointed at a line at the bottom of Donny Tiffany's confession statement.

Donny, as if forgetting his anguish said, "Miss

Stanforth teached me how to write my name in fifth grade." He took the pen and, in sloppy, jittering cursive, Donny Tiffany signed his future away.

—

"They made Rube the chief shortly after Shawnie Gosselin went missing in July. Then he blamed the kidnapping and then murders of the final girl in 'eighty-three on a transient who was shot while being taken into custody," Sylvain said.

"Convenient," Nick said.

"They just—"

Sylvain waved a hand high above his head, shouting, interrupting Jaqi. "Leroy! Hey, did you hear about Charlaine Chabot?" He creaked to his feet and started away in an old man shamble, as if he'd forgotten he was in the middle of a conversation.

Nick and Jaqi watched him go. The man reached a bench where another retiree sat. His voice carried and it was as if he was replaying a conversation he'd only just had.

"Well, that was something," Jaqi said.

Nick took her hand. "Come on, let's get this done. I'm getting hungry already."

"Should've packed a lunch," Jaqi said, teasing.

They again started across the gravel lot. The sun was reaching for the midday spot in the sky. All around them, life went on as if girls weren't being kidnapped, raped, murdered, and then disposed of in disgusting fashion.

9

"So, you haven't seen her?" Renee Sparks said, hope all but gone. "Right. Well. Do you know, has she been seeing someone—no, I understand. Thanks. If you hear from her, tell her to call home."

She cradled the phone receiver and leaned her forehead against the wall next to the fridge. She'd gotten home a little after 6:00 AM. Exhausted, she'd washed her face and went to bed. At around noon, she climbed from bed. She visited the can, then the kitchen, calling out to her daughter as she went. The door to a slim patio and a weedy backyard was slightly ajar. On the floor next to the door was an oval of glass about the size of a softball.

Wrong, wrong, wrong.

She'd called out again as she hurried to her daughter's bedroom. After telling herself to keep calm, she snatched Melissa's diary, which had become more of an address book with extra pages for doodling. The last entry was nine months prior. One of her friends had come to school in a T-bar thong, whale tails riding up onto the bulges of her slight love handles, and all the boys had stared whenever the girl bent forward, which she'd spent much of the day doing. Didn't matter, completely normal teenaged girl behavior. What mattered were the eleven names and phone numbers of Melissa's close friends.

Renee had called them all, then called two past boyfriends and Melissa's chemistry tutor, then, finally, the girl's boss. Nobody had seen her since yesterday.

"It's nothing. It's just a precaution," she said after dialing the number to the police station, one eye pinned to that oval of glass she dared not touch.

The line clicked and a whiny, feminine voice said, "Delson Police Department, is this an emergency?"

"Maybe. My daughter didn't come home and the back door's open and there's this piece of cut glass. I phoned her friends and work, and I called her tutor and—"

"Cut glass? Ma'am, please hold."

Within a handful of seconds, an officer named Markus Tolvanen took the call, listened to the rundown, then put Renee Sparks back on hold. As she waited, elevator muzak in her ear, she tried to will her daughter's presence into being. Six times she played a fantasy of her daughter stepping through the door, explaining away the absence, the cut glass, the open door, her absolute safety.

Renee was so lost in reverie that she didn't hear a click or the music stop.

"Mrs. Sparks? Hello?"

"Yes?"

"Two officers are on their way to your home. Please, don't touch anything."

Renee took a shuddering breath. "It's not him. He's not back. Right? It's not him?"

"Officers are on their way."

The receiver slipped from Renee's hand, thunking heavily on the linoleum. She pressed her forehead to the wall and began to pray to a god she hadn't believed in since childhood. When no solace came from that, she tried all the gods she could think of, despite knowing she was an evolved ape, spinning on a rock in the middle of an endless mat of cold, black universe.

10

The first time Melissa awoke, she'd had a headache so big and physically debilitating, she wished she were dead and got the next best thing: she passed out, whether from exhaustion or mental self-preservation did not matter. Now, though, the headache was down to a dull throb. It allowed her to acknowledge how much her face stung. She tasted blood from a split lip and a bitten tongue. She opened her eyes as she jerked forward, recalling the man who had come from her bedroom shadows.

Now, she was in a squat room featuring wood-paneled walls and ceiling. And not the cheap stuff, though still softwood, it looked thick and sturdy. The door was steel and had an oversized mail slot in the middle where, currently, a plate of bright orange noodles and a glass bottle of milk with a nipple lid sat on a folded-out ledge. Melissa didn't dare touch it, though she did rise from the too soft mattress.

The floor was stained grey cement and cool beneath her bare feet. Her guts burbled. She scanned around again and saw, next to the springy cot, was a five-gallon Valvoline Oil pail, a toilet seat resting on top. Her chin began to quiver as she clenched her asshole. It made her guts dance worse. She had no choice.

"Please!" the shout came out like a frog's croak; it also dislodged something within. She pulled down her pants and sat heavily on the bucket. Instantly a hot wash of waste burst free. Tears spilled steadily down her cheeks as she dug fingernails into her milky thighs. Thankfully, there was a fresh roll of toilet paper sitting between her left heel and the bucket.

Settled and waiting to see if there was more, she again looked about the room for some kind of opening to exploit. There was a shelf with a row of books—the brunt of which were focussed on the topic of pregnancy—and an extra roll of toilet paper. Everything smelled musty and dated, not so different from when she and her cousins used to play in her grandmother's basement as kids. It smelled like that because of a lack of traffic.

Nobody came for the other girls, why would they come for her?

"Help! Please!"

There was no question of where she was, no denying

it either. He had her; the Delson Dollmaker had her. He raped girls and killed them after doing their makeup and nails, or maybe he did the makeup and nails after; Melissa didn't recall.

She did know she didn't want to be in this vulnerable position when the freak came for her. Quickly, she wiped and closed the lid. She went to the cot and hid beneath the blankets for close to five minutes—not that she was counting. She then shifted from the cot. Maybe the Dollmaker was feeling too confident and as a result, made a mistake or two.

She glared at the shiny doorknob. She wouldn't know unless she tried. She broke for the door like it had been open and was now closing. The knob was cold. She twisted, she pulled, the door did not budge, not even when she bounced a shoulder off its sturdy surface.

"Fuck," she hissed, the word gravelly and yet phlegmy.

She'd have to get the better of him, meaning she needed a weapon. She looked back at the cot. The frame was heavy and steel. The fasteners were bulged rivets rather than bolts—there'd be no twisting free any of the steel. She bent lower while on her knees and peered into the shadows beneath the cot.

It took a moment for her vision to adjust. To understand just what she was looking at. A panicked panting began, rising from her chest, sucking all the oxygen from her system.

Dear god.

There were grey bars in a small section of the wall about two-feet wide. Behind those bars was a tight cavity, a cell. What Melissa saw forced free a scream that seemed to threaten tearing her vocal chords from their mounts. Behind her, the door opened.

"Don't worry about that under there. Behave and you'll be fine," said a vaguely familiar voice.

Melissa began to shake. She couldn't turn away from what she saw, couldn't look at the Dollmaker; a small voice inside told her, *if you can't identify him, maybe he'll let you go…eventually.*

11

They'd spent $8.45 on nickel photocopies from various books, out-of-town newspapers, and maps at the library. Thanks to the librarian and her small team, everything was exactly where it should've been. Nick found the necessary cards in the catalogs, then Jaqi played gopher. The newspapers the librarian brought out in huge leather scrapbooks based on years, printed by the newspapers' shared publisher.

"Guess it makes sense The Sun and The Star would have the same printer, both being from Toronto," Jaqi said absently.

The librarian flipped open the front page and pointed to the information sheet. "Yes, but both are printed in North Bay. I don't recall which, but one of those two has a physical press of their own, but it's more profitable to print for local businesses and send their mass needs up north."

"Really?" Jaqi said, leaning in to read the publishing information that did indeed state the tome was printed in North Bay, Ontario. "Huh."

The librarian spoke mostly when directly addressed but she was there next to them and willing to assist in using the new Xerox machine. According to her, they'd had the same machine before that for seven years, and had color not come to be a necessity, they likely would've used it seven more years.

"Try to imagine an electronic machine lasting even seven years now," she said, gently stroking the molded plastic edge of the boxy scanner/copier/fax machine.

They'd learned, about an hour after stepping inside, that the old man named Sylvain had been telling everyone he met the story of Delson's chief of police, Robert Thompson—or Rube, Rube the Tractor Tube—for more than a decade, likely over parking tickets he'd received. Though, when they asked if Donny Tiffany was railroaded, the librarian only cringed.

"I really don't know enough about the situation to say," she said, and before there was a chance to add to it, four books thumped through the return slot from outside and she buzzed off behind the main desk.

Jaqi looked to Nick, but he only shrugged. They finished up and by the end had a huge stack of pages.

—

The maps went up onto the rented walls of their apartment. Colored thumbtacks drove into the drywall everywhere where a victim was taken from, everywhere a victim had lived, and finally, where the bodies surfaced. This included the five dead girls from more than a decade ago, just in case.

"What are the chances multiple serial killers hunt Delson?" Nick had said when Jaqi asked if they should mark those first five victims.

She could only scrunch her mouth.

They sat on the couch, eating McCain fries with Heinz ketchup and salt, staring at the maps as if they held a code to decipher. Delson didn't grow into more than a village until the automobile was commonplace in most households, meaning the streets looked rational from above: simple crisscrossing lines. The thumbtacks, while slightly clustered, didn't appear to show any signs of pattern. The dumping sites were the most sporadic, though it was obvious each body was to be recovered quickly—why else would a man *doll* them up?

After more then five minutes of study, Nick said, "So, where do we start?"

Jaqi plucked an overcooked little fry and popped it into her mouth, crunching away as she said, "I suppose we go talk to the neighbors. Doubt we'll get through everybody before the weekend's over."

Nick bounced his head, left-right, left-right. "Maybe. I'm guessing most people won't feel like talking, or they'll feel like they've said everything there is to say."

"I doubt it. People love to talk," Jaqi said, then plucked another little brown fry from their shared plate.

"We'll see. There's talking to make sound and there's talking that means something."

Jaqi turned her attention back to the wall. "Real question is, do we say we're from the Mirror, or do we say we're freelancing?"

Nick frowned with his entire upper body. "Well, they'd probably fire me if they thought it was…you know what, fuck it." Nick rose and stepped into the kitchen with his empty plate and the ketchup bottle.

Jaqi followed him, bringing her dirty plate and empty glass. "Who you calling?"

"Marcel," Nick said, flipping to the R section of his address book. He punched the number and waited, receiver pinched between his shoulder and ear. "Hi, may I speak with Marcel?"

Jaqi rinsed her plate, then Nick's. Anything to keep her busy. Nick hated people looking at him when he was on the phone, as if the information couldn't wait even one damned second for him to hang up. Jaqi had learned that the first time she'd asked him a question when he was on the line with Domino's Pizza. He'd given her a look that etched itself on her mind.

"Hey, Marcel, Nick Price here, I was just wondering if you had plans of canning me. I know you're interviewing—" Nick nodded twice, then snorted. "Come on, man. Why you bullshitting—"

Jaqi set the plates and her glass in the ancient, moderately reliable dishwasher. She busied her hands with a dishtowel, only glancing to Nick's back. He didn't have many foibles—that she knew of—and the phone thing was likely the most prominent.

"Uh huh. Okay. In the future, next time you're firing someone, just do it." Nick hung up the phone. He tsked, irritation clear on his face. "He says I can work the next week, scanning old newspapers in order to digitize them."

"That's perfect," Jaqi said. "Well, pretty good, anyway. We can say we're with the paper and the worst thing your boss can do is speed up the inevitable."

"Fuck him. Also, I'm going to tell off that pregnant cunt next time I see her."

Jaqi smiled widely, placing her hands on Nick's shoulder, moving her face to about six inches from his. "That's the spirit. Let's go ask some questions," she said and pecked him on the lips.

—

"Did you see anybody out of place around the time your neighbor went missing?" Jaqi said, she held a tape recorder in one hand and a closed legal pad with a pen through the spiraling plastic spine.

"Ah, well, like I told the cops, I don't recall seeing anybody out of place," the man said.

He wore blue slacks with myriad patches, scuffed brown boots, and a Maple Leafs cap that didn't quite cover the fact he was completely bald up top, though kept a ring of hair from the tips of his ears down to the top of his neck. This was a next-door neighbor to Elise Tabaracci; she went missing in June last year and her body was discovered in July. She was the first to go missing of last year's crop of victims and had the second shortest stint of being MIA. Police found her in a red and white polka dot dress, her nails done in red—both fingers and toes—her makeup tastefully applied, her hair dyed two shades lighter than was natural. The police kept most of any evidence they'd found behind tight lips, or perhaps they hadn't found enough to discuss.

"Who would you consider *in place*?" Nick said.

The man thought a moment, hand cupping his chin. "Well, I suppose all the neighbors here, but the street's not a shortcut to anything, nothing like that, so…could be the ice cream truck came by. It does most days in the summer. I don't know, there's a couple Mary Kay ladies who have kind of hilarious turf wars in town."

"Mary Kay, as in makeup?" Nick said, eyebrows high as they'd go.

The man must've pieced the connection. "Hold a sec'," he said before jogging in through his open garage door. Within a minute, he was on his way back, a woman in jeans and a faded Blue Jays t-shirt by his side. "This is my wife."

"Doug says you want to know about the Mary Kay women?" The wife held out two business cards. "I buy from Gayle there, but only 'cause I've known her so long.

I got a makeover once from this Dini girl and she's much more with the current styles. If Dini was fixing my face every morning instead of me, I'd buy from her. I used to buy everything from Maryanne LeBeau, but that was forever ago. She was the queen of pushing Mary Kay." She closed her eyes. "LeBeau? Labanc, maybe. LeBeau…that was forever ago. You think this is somehow related to the Dollmaker?"

The words spilled from the woman in a lava flow of mostly useless information. It took both Nick and Jaqi a few moments to reconcile all that was said.

Jaqi got it first and said, "It's unlikely, but this is a community piece, everything is important."

Nick nodded. They hadn't gone over any of that, but it's exactly what he'd pictured: a small city shaken to its core, the citizens left to sift through the rubble like the survivors of a deadly earthquake.

"What happened to those girls has an impact on the entire community, don't you think?" Nick said. Jaqi was gung-ho, sure, but she wasn't exactly adept at asking the kind of questions that produced meaningful, impactful quotes. In her defense, she was more about acquiring the entire picture of things.

The husband and wife both nodded eagerly before speaking simultaneously. Nature selected its winner and the husband quieted to let the woman wax a little less than poetic closing out with "…we all feel 'real, 'real bad about those girls. I know everyone imagines they were their own girls. Just breaks my heart."

Smiling, Nick thanked the pair. He led Jaqi over to the home on the far side of the Tabaracci place—which was currently on the market with Century21.

"Make sure you ask open-ended questions, nothing where a simple yes or no covers it," Nick said, speaking almost into Jaqi's shoulder as the woman they'd come to see was already standing on the stone path that led to her front door, waiting for them.

—

"It's not very busy around here, but that means nothing. Nothing. Follow me," the woman said, leading Nick and Jaqi around to the back of the house. The yards lined up, subtly different fences demarcating each property. Beams of light cut between many of the slats, fighting a losing battle against the thick shadows. Beyond the fences was a slim street. "This is one of the original streets. There's a few places in town like this, where the garbage trucks roll by but nobody pays attention to them." Beyond the slim street were the backyards of another row of houses. "You know, I been thinking, and I decided it has to be someone going around unseen."

"You think…" Jaqi began, trailing, then rewording. "Aside from that garbagemen go unnoticed, what else makes you think one's capable of such a thing."

Nick smirked, side eying Jaqi. For some reason, she wanted this more than he did, and he had a pretty big reason to want it. With her, it was more like an impulse.

"I don't know, but the only other jobs I can think of where they're around and nobody sees them are cops and the ice cream truck. Guess those are the ones that get seen. But I know it isn't the ice cream truck; my cousin Randy's a good boy, everything they say about him is bull."

"Perfect, we were hoping to speak with the ice cream truck driver. Any chance you could give us his number?" Nick said.

The woman scowled. "He's a good boy. I don't know what you think, but that girl was a doggone liar."

Nick plastered a winning smile on his face. "Of course, but he might've seen the Dollmaker and didn't realize. He is around a lot."

"Well, okay," the woman said, then rattled off Ronald Adams' name and phone number.

As they were walking to the houses across the street where a litter of bicycles rose from a pristine green lawn like a herpes sore from an otherwise unblemished lip, Jaqi said, "They'd have looked into Ronald."

"No doubt. I bet they grilled him, checked his alibi, then tried to prove it wrong. I'm no expert, but a guy like that feels too obvious, if they haven't gotten him already. He drives an ice cream truck, he's not one of these guys who can pay their way out of evidence." Nick led them up onto a concrete porch, then rang the doorbell.

Jaqi pointed to an older, more scuffed bicycle in the mound. "My next-door neighbor had a bike just like that when I was growing up."

—

"I heard he raped his grandma up the poop chute."

"Yeah, me too."

Six boys sat on the floor or a couch in a cramped and Doritos-smelling living room, watching another boy battle mummies, scarabs, demons, blobs, and a series of undefinable enemies in an epileptic's nightmare. The boys all looked to be around twelve years old. A couple said little, but the others said anything that came to their heads; obviously Nick and Jaqi didn't fit into the category of adults needing to be minded.

"Forget Ronald a minute," Nick said. "You see anybody weird hanging around the neighborhood last summer, before Elise was taken?"

Five boys shrugged in near unison. The sixth boy kept his eyes on the screen—a floating head was now telling the kid with the controller that it was time for the next bad guy, and that if he won, he could fight the floating head himself—despite that he wasn't playing.

"What about you? Did you see anybody?" Nick said to the kid.

He looked at Nick and Jaqi, then opened his mouth before quickly closing it.

Nick leaned in, sensing something juicy was forthcoming. "It's okay."

"Muh-muh-my da-dad says it's a-a-a cuh-cop do-do-doing ih-it."

Ignoring speech impediments was something one of his college profs had pounded home in him, suggesting that when it came to quote the individual, to do so in a positive light. 'You also have to listen. One of the best scoops I ever received was from a man who could hardly talk.' What the professor hadn't mentioned, but Nick figured was true: treating them as if nothing was different would almost certainly embolden them, create comfort, aid in spilling whatever beans needed spilled. At least he hoped so.

"Maybe if the crime was committed at Tim Hortons," one boy said.

"Do you live near any of the victims, and have you seen cops around more than usual?" Nick said, ignoring the snarky comment, attention focussed on the kid with the impediment.

"Uh-uh-I luh-luh-luh," the kid paused, then started anew, "I fucking live fucking a fucking block away fruh-fruh-from fucking Pheobe fucking Huddy."

The kid playing, without shifting his body an iota, enrapt by the game, said, "He can talk better if he swears."

"Oh, well, that can't be too fucking convenient in class," Nick said.

The boys laughed and the kid with the impediment smiled widely enough to reveal a set of deeply yellow teeth, plaque built like coral reefs at the edges of his gums. Evidently, the speech issues were likely just another item in a list this kid's guardians were neglecting.

—

They interviewed people until stopping into Pizza Delight for supper and a couple cold bottles of Old Vienna beer. The place had a dated vibe, but the food was excellent and the staff were efficient and personable.

"I didn't know they still sold this," Jaqi said, lifting

and looking at the label on her weepy beer bottle. "My grandfather used to drink this. This town's a bit of a time warp. That bike. This beer."

"Not bad, though," Nick said.

Jaqi set down the bottle next to her greasy plate. "You know, we might actually figure out a few real, I mean really real suspects."

"You're into this, huh?"

She sat back, hands folded onto her lap. "I think I am. I'm totally surprised, but I just keep thinking if we get back out there, we can build this fantastic story, and maybe figure out something the cops missed. If there's *any* truth to what that old man said in the library parking lot, the Delson PD is a bunch of dough-heads."

"One of my greatest surprises since starting college and interviewing people is just how dumb most cops really seem to be. Though some play coy."

"Yeah, well, there's no stopping us now. Doesn't matter how smart the cops are," Jaqi said, picking at food between her teeth as she spoke.

"All right," Nick said. "All right, we'll keep interviewing. Go through the entire phonebook until there's nobody left to quote. Will have to grab some more tapes. We'll have to be smart, they don't cost much, but they cost—"

Jaqi waved this away. "Come off it. We both know who'll pay for the tapes."

Nick did know, but rarely did he directly mention the money she received from her father, money that just kept coming, as long as Jaqi remained in school, working toward a degree—then doctorate, if her father got his way.

"Is he paying for dessert?" Nick said, then plucked free the little menu that had been nestled between a napkin holder and refillable Heinz Ketchup bottle.

12

Ronald was of average height and build, but he was soft and pale in a way that brought to mind gelatinous things: used pan grease, infection buildup, deepwater slugs. He was the first stop of the morning; Randy had warned them the night before that he had to get his truck ready bright and early and be on the street by 11:00 AM. When Jaqi was about to suggest they come at 6:00 AM, Randy saved her breath by demanding they get to his place first thing...sometime between 9:30 and 10:00 AM.

There they were, sitting in his basement apartment; a foot away, a cigarette constantly smoldering in a big glass ashtray. The place reeked of spent tobacco, ash mounds, and adult male body odor. A rank recipe. Randy's right index and middle finger, as well as the pad of his right thumb, were deeply yellowed from smoking. Brown streaks dripped down the walls, remnants of an indoor smoker lacking the energy, will, or awareness to know things needed cleaned now and then. Randy, in his element, would've made a fine anti-smoking campaign, or perhaps a stay in school campaign.

"They kept me in there all night 'til they talked to my cousin Jonny and the bartender down there at The Rooster. I was visiting Jonny the night the second chick went missing. On the third one I was in the fucking drunk tank! They came at me over this goddamned tomato who was fourteen going on thirty. Wasn't like I forced her. I even paid her twenty bucks. Little bitch was a junkie. Should've been her parents getting charged, not me. She weren't no virgin when I had her."

"Right, wild. So, you're around a lot, did you see anything out of place near any of the victims' homes?" Nick said. "We're only here because you and the ice cream truck are kind of a staple on those blocks come summer."

Jaqi had matching fists held tightly below view thanks to a table. Her jaws clenched, her eyes stony.

"Me and the Dollmaker, huh? I think it's a cop doing it. Only people I seent around all the time. The cops go anywhere, and nobody don't notice a thing. Some idiots even feel safe when cops come 'round. Morons."

Nick glanced at Jaqi. Two unrelated people mentioning the police felt a little—admittedly very little—like it might be something. All stories were built on a foundation of somethings. Unfortunately, most easily found somethings had nothing to do with a story's foundation.

"Which cops?" Nick said.

"All them."

"Ah, okay. Did you see anything else, perhaps during a break. You know, you get out, walk around a—"

"Can't get out on the job. My parole officer had to work to get it where I could even be near kids if I'm in a big fucking van. That little whore said she was older. I met her in the Tilton Hilton for fuck sakes. What was she doing there if she ain't old enough?" Randy ashed his cigarette aggressively over one of the loaded ashtrays within arm's reach. "How am I the one getting shit when she's fourteen and drinking in a bar?"

"Damned mystery, that," Nick said.

—

"I need a shower," Jaqi said the moment they stepped out of the man's home. "Imagine that guy selling ice cream to kids." She convulsed as if gagging up a mouthful of bile. "Imagine that guy climbing on top of you…at fourteen." She shook her head slowly. "This town just about deserves a serial killer."

Nick cringed. "You hungry, hon?"

Jaqi spun on her heels, a finger pointed with deadly intent at Nick. "That goddamned scumbag. Imagine that loser saying, saying," she stamped her right foot on the asphalt, "saying anything about anyone!"

"Babe, that's going to happen, we're going to talk to scumbags."

The finger remained firm. "I want to name the fucking creep who killed those girls. I want to name him and watch a judge sentence him to a hole for the rest of his miserable life."

"Or *her*," Nick said.

The severity of the pointing finger wilted until curling, seemingly bringing her arm down to her side with it. "If it's the same guy as fifteen years ago, then in fifteen years he'll probably do it again. Somebody must know something." There was moisture behind the words.

Nick gathered her in his arms. "Maybe the story we put together will start a domino effect. One person thinks of something, then another and another, then it's over, and we helped make it so."

Jaqi sighed against his chest. "There was a girl taken from my school when I was in second grade; she was in kindergarten. I haven't thought about that in years."

"Really?" Nick said.

"Yeah. It turned out to be her estranged dad, and she came back to school after a while, but for a few days it was important. We had an assembly where police came in to tell us to avoid strangers, and if we couldn't find our parents, police would always help."

Nick pushed her out to an arm's length. "You know, as unlikely as it seems, a cop really could roam around a neighborhood unnoticed, or at least, unacknowledged."

Jaqi let go of Nick's hips. "I wish—well, I don't really wish, but, like, I wish I grew up here; it feels like this should be easy to figure out. I mean, he has to be local, right?"

Nick rubbed Jaqi's forearms. "He has to be pretty

damned familiar, if he's not."

"Or they."

After thirty uncounted seconds passed, Nick said, "Want to hit the chip wagon?"

—

The chip wagon was a permanent fixture out front of the defunct Pontiac/Jeep/Eagle dealership and repair shop. To the side of the wagon—a refitted caravan trailer—were two picnic tables. The tables were stained and grey, marred by hundreds of messages carved into their surfaces. The chip wagon itself looked no better. Grease oozed from around the vents, the fan hanging next to the order window was caked with fuzzy black grime, and the vinyl exterior was faded and cracked, and in some places featured strips of weathered duct tape that was peeling and stringy. The woman who ran the place—Donna Reid—looked decades older than her age. She had grey and black hair, slightly curly, very fuzzy, and always hanging just over the food. A cigarette burned perpetually from the corner of her mouth. She was rail thin and had a voice like gravel in a cement mixer.

She was leaning out the order window, talking to a couple farmer-looking types—guys with big arms, big bellies, and big appetites. They both had balled tinfoil wrappers before them and then another wrapper beneath second burgers on the go. Their cardboard fry containers were empty but for ketchup smears and salt grains.

Jaqi stepped up to the meagre menu while Nick went to the window. Donna didn't so much as glance his way.

"Do they think it's the Dollmaker?" Donna said, excitement thrumming through her words.

"What's this?" Nick said, half-turning to ask all in attendance.

"Girl named Melissa Sparks has gone missing," the older of the men said.

"How do they know it was *him*?" Jaqi said, moving to stand next to Nick, her hands wrapping around his arm.

"Cops ain't saying much yet, but I hear the window on the back door was used to gain entry. I heard he cuts the glass, but they're leaving it out of the story, to…you know…get him."

"And Melissa Sparks isn't a runaway type," the younger man said. "My brother knows her. She's a few years younger. Used to date this kid who helped with haying the last few years. He used to complain how she always went home at the end of the night and she never gave him…" the man trailed, his cheeks flushed.

Jaqi squeezed against Nick. He leaned into her, sharing one another's warmth and proximity. For Nick, this story idea suddenly felt a whole lot more important than it had. And not only for his future.

"Wish they'd find the guy," Donna said.

"Wish they'd get their goddamned heads out of their asses," the younger man said.

"Wish somebody would look into the cops; has to be a reason he's not been caught yet," the older man said.

Nick whispered, "Third times a charm?"

"Maybe," Jaqi whispered back.

13

Sunday nights The Bruce closed at 10:00 PM. Aside from Lexy Mallette behind the bar, the entire crowd was four men posted up on stools—the regulars. Zach and Kris were excited, angry even. Andrei and Colin were somber, though did not seem opposed to hatching some kind of plan to catch the freak.

"Obviously it has to be one of us who catches this fuck," Zach said. "Hasn't been a half-decent cop in town since you quit."

Kris huffed. "Got that right. Those assholes. You know, they fired me because I was doing too good a job," he said.

Kris didn't make it through the three-month probation period. Four different assault complaints sealed his fate as a boy in blue. That was back in 1981; Kris had been twenty-one.

"That or you kept beating on people," Lexy said, eying the man, daring him to challenge what she said. Lexy's brother was beaten unconscious for refusing to exit his car after being pulled over for doing six clicks above the posted speed limit.

Zach waved a drunken arm. "Who wasn't excitable in his early twenties? Your brother was speeding…"

Lexy nodded. "And you're visibly drunk, therefore I can no longer serve you."

Andrei laughed, smile sticking around long after Kris and Zach sneered his way.

"How we going to catch this fuck?" Colin said.

Making it obvious about to whom he spoke, Zach said, "We should take this to my garage. Don't know that we can trust every set of ears in here."

Lexy rolled her eyes and went back to the battered paperback copy of *Sphere* by Michael Crichton she was reading between grabbing beers.

"Tonight?" Andrei said, cringing.

Zach waved both arms this time. "Hell no. Tomorrow night—"

"No good. My youngest's got a ballgame," Kris said.

"Okay, Tuesday—" Zach said, red-faced, words sloppy.

"Can't do it," Colin said. "I'm pulling double routes because Gerry's going to the city with his wife."

"Tell him to drive his own—"

Colin cut Zach off. "Man, they're going to discuss treatment options for her cancer."

Zach deflated. "Oh, come on. How would I know that?" Nobody said a thing in response. "How about Wednesday or Thursday?"

"Thursday's better than Wednesday," Kris said.

"Fine with me," Colin said.

Andrei shrugged "All right, but I don't know about this. If something unexpected happens, we're liable.

Police can screw up, but we can't, especially not with something like this."

All three men spied Andrei with slitted eyes.

"So, what, you're out?" Zach said as Kris said, "You don't wanna catch this sicko?"

Andrei pushed from his stool. "I want to see this man caught. I want to see him get what's coming. I'm willing to try; we just have to be careful…maybe lay off the brews a bit if we're going to do this."

"If?" Zach said. "I'm all the way in, and when I catch this motherfucker, he's going to get every bit of treatment he gave those poor girls. He sure as shit won't make it to court unscathed."

Lexy looked up from her book, grimace on her face. A moment later, the cook stepped through the swinging door with a trey of freshly dish-washed glasses and mugs. He set the trey down on the bar top with a clatter. Nobody was talking, each man focussed on his drink, Lexy focussed on her shoes.

"Somebody die?" the cook said, when nobody answered, he put a hand on Lexy's shoulder. "I'm all done. Heading home now, unless you need me to stick around."

Lexy side-eyed the patrons, then leaned in to whisper in the cook's ear. The cook nodded, then hurried back the way he'd come.

Four seconds passed.

"How long you two been fucking?" Zach said.

Lexy turned beet red.

14

Martine was looking green when Nick stepped into the breakroom to deposit his sack lunch in the freshly cleaned fridge. She held a water cup just above her enlarged bosom, as if catching her breath between chugs. She also looked exhausted and sore.

"If it ain't Mr. Balls," Martine said, her upper lip slightly curled.

Nick, mind so glued to the Delson Dollmaker, could only look at the woman in confusion and continue through the motions of his morning.

Eugene stepped into the breakroom, yawning. "Morning."

"Morning," Nick said.

Martine acted as if her co-worker hadn't stepped into the room. "So, you know you're not long for the Mirror, and thank god. You should've been fired—"

"If your kid comes out half as ugly as your personality, he'll always have a job with the circus open to him." Nick poured a mug of coffee from the pot already more than half-empty, faced away from Martine.

Eugene laughed a single, hearty bark. Nick turned and looked at his soon to be ex-coworkers. The sneer on

Martine's face was enough to keep Nick from benefitting from his joke much. Then she straightened and smiled at him.

"Enjoy the basement; it's dark and damp and smelly, likely reminds you of your childhood."

Nick wrinkled his expression. "My childhood."

Martine tipped her head, laying the attitude on thickly. "Yeah, from your days living under troll bridges with your troll family."

"Wap waaap," Eugene intoned nasally.

"Hey, fuck you," Martine said. "This kid *is* a joke. How he graduated college…must be pretty low standards these days."

Now Nick did laugh. He raised his mug in cheers, then started away. He didn't bother with his desk, instead went to the basement where the big scanner was set up on an old Apple. Up until January of 1996, the Mirror had pasted each page of newspaper they released in huge scrapbooks with leather covers—much like the nice omnibuses of The Sun and The Star he'd scanned from at the library. Nick guessed he was expected to begin in the 1920s, where the provincially funded summer students left off last year. There'd been no funding this year, according to what Marcel had said a few months back—when Nick had been on better terms—so the work had ceased, despite it needing done and the need coming from a real social sense of value. It was impossible to say when someone would need to comb through back issues of the newspaper.

And, of course, Nick wanted to do just that.

He located the leatherbound book containing every page of news printed in 1982. A grunt escaped him as he pulled the massive tome off the shelf. The scent of must and the taste of mildew hit him with enough strength to force his head away in a jerk. He set the book down on the big wooden table, and flipped it open to the first page.

The lead story was about a New Year's Eve party that had been held at the Legion. The picture was taken outside a single story building with wood siding. Nick tried to think of where the building was located and couldn't, then understood part of it when he made out the park next-door. That Legion building was gone, perhaps on purpose, perhaps by accident, he didn't know. He did know, however, that a newish medical clinic was there now, next to that same park.

"Learn something new every day," he said as he folded back the steel arms of the bite-like mechanisms that kept the pages in place. Once all three were open, he could slide a page free. The mechanisms reminded him of Duo-Tang folders he used in middle school, though these were much, much bigger and much, much heartier.

The sheet went onto the scanner, then Nick awoke the hibernating computer. It took about four minutes for the damned thing to work through the process of coming to. The scanner was loud. Light blasted free around the cracks as it played down the page.

By the time the first sheet was scanned, Nick had all the pages out. He flipped the first page over and clicked

START to begin scanning. After a sip of coffee, he made stacks of pages, then thumbed through the second until he hit May. If the murderer in 1982 had anything to do with the Dollmaker, he'd almost certainly be hunting girls during the warmer months. Everything they'd been able to piece together suggested serial killers followed their own set of patterns.

May turned up nothing, but June 2 did. A seventeen-year-old named Gloria Bacon was taken from her backyard where she'd been lying on a blanket, watching the stars. A bag of marijuana had been discovered next to the blanket; Gloria's parents were adamant that it *had* to belong to the person who'd taken her.

Different pleas for Gloria's safe return appeared throughout the following three issues of the Mirror—in 1982, the paper still ran regular editions Monday and Wednesday, then a chunky issue every Sunday; in 1997, the paper came out on Wednesdays and Sundays, and neither issue was ever particularly chunky.

By the fourth issue after the disappearance, the obvious became facts: the weed had been Gloria's, the girl wasn't as goodie-goodie as her parents had assumed, and that whoever had her, wasn't in it for a ransom, as no contact had been made, meaning no demands or offers. The girl was gone without a trace.

Nick continued scanning and reading. He decided the Gloria Bacon case was close enough to make use of the printer also attached to the computer. The printed page came out shrunken, impossible to read down there in the dim light, but Jaqi would figure out some device to take it in.

The way she was becoming attached to this story—and he assumed with his future—was somewhat alarming. There was no chance even half of her drive was because she wanted him to do well. This story had its claws in her. An obsession.

By the end of June, Gloria Bacon was no longer a vital topic. Her family still made pleas, as did her friends and the police, but everything appeared near the rear and below the fold, surrounded by classifieds and notices. This was not where news went to be seen, it was where news filled in the spaces the ads weren't.

August 4, 1982 featured the first appearance of Teresa Brooke. Her parents had left her home to babysit her brother—fourteen and severely handicapped, both physically and mentally—for a rare night out. They returned from dinner and a movie to find their son in wet diapers and unfed, and the back door had been forced open—how it was forced was left from the report. They also discovered their daughter was missing.

Nick continued scanning and flipping, making copies of pertinent pages. By the time he finally shot a glance at his watch, it was well after eleven o'clock and his hands looked as if he'd been playing in a coalbin. He straightened out his spine, grabbed his empty coffee mug, then headed upstairs. Keyboards clacked and ad salespeople chattered on the phones. Though he couldn't explain why, Nick dreaded seeing anyone in the breakroom. If he could, he'd come and go for the rest of the week in quiet invisibility. Getting fired plain sucked.

The breakroom was empty. He sighed.

He looked at the coffee pot.

Empty. He sighed again.

He dumped two bulbous scoops of fresh grounds over the morning pot's grounds in the basket, then filled the pot from the tap. Once the water bubbled up and then down into the pot, he pulled his sack lunch from the fridge and fished out the baggy of cheese and crackers he'd packed. He made two little sandwiches, the golden, flaky exteriors of the Ritz crackers darkened by the ink from his fingers.

"How goes the battle?" Marcel said, stepping into the breakroom, as was his way whenever he heard a fresh pot of coffee burbling and dripping into creation. "Two students were at it all summer and only got through five years."

Nick huffed. With only one scanner, it was barely enough work for just him—and if he wasn't reading up on past crimes, he'd be bored senseless down there.

"Should've put them to work at different times. It's hardly a one-man job," Nick said.

Marcel put his hands up in a *not my doing* gesture. "Government paid. Besides, one of them always made sure the coffee was going."

"Probably to break up the monotony of scanning," Nick said after swallowing the last bite of his snack.

"Pretty boring, is it?" Marcel said.

Nick backpedaled. "Not for me. I'm reading lots that I'm scanning."

Marcel pointed a finger gun at Nick, though he seemed surprised. "That'll make the job bearable, I guess."

Nick did some quick mental calculations and understood. Marcel had put him on this task to make him quit so he wouldn't need to officially fire him. He nearly laughed; this job was exactly what he needed to be doing right now.

Though the coffeepot was only two-thirds full, Nick rose to pour himself a cup. "Yep, and don't worry, I'll be here 'til you officially fire me." He winked.

Marcel said nothing in reply, turning to busy himself with the contents of the cupboard above the sink.

15

Jaqi wore a pair of boxer shorts and a ratty t-shirt from a camp where she'd worked as a counselor the summer before her first year of university. She'd been looking over the notes and replaying snippets of audio from the ever-growing mound of tapes. They'd now spoken with twenty-six locals, many sharing property lines with one of the murdered or missing girls. Most of it seemed like bullshit, but the cop thing demanded her attention like an angry hangnail.

Nick had suggested it might be a misstep to consider Pierre Allard, former lawyer turned cop, as an ally, but Jaqi figured it would hardly change things for the worse if she called him. And, really, she needed to call him. Considering what they'd gathered, and its quality, they'd need any inside help they could get, even just to get themselves pointed in the right direction. And it wasn't about doing well; the need to find this guy was significantly stronger than any need—aside from bodily needs—that she'd ever felt. Compelled, she felt utterly compelled.

"Delson Police Department, is this an emergency?"

"No," Jaqi said. "Can you put me through to extension twenty-three?"

"Of course, have a nice day."

"You t—" Jaqi stopped abruptly, hearing the click preceding a pulse when she was mid-word.

"Hello, you have reached the desk of Constable Pierre Allard. Please, leave a message at the appropriate time."

The phone beeped into Jaqi's ear, and she quickly said, "This is Jaqi Bazinet. I was wondering if you could help me with something wholly unrelated to stabbing men..." As she rattled off the phone number at the apartment, she cringed at her joke, deciding it was miles from funny and that the man would never call her.

"Oh well," she said, setting the receiver back into its cradle and returning to the map. She and Nick had rented a few catch a killer kind of movies to figure what clues might lead to what, but the only one that felt grounded in a semblance of realistic investigation was *Silence of the Lambs*. Quoting as best as she could recall, Jaqi whispered, "He covets, and what does he covet? He covets what he sees every day." After this line was said, she whispered it internally like a mantra off and on through the night. Now it was there, and if Pierre Allard didn't have anything for her, she at least had her search narrowed…maybe.

The victim locations meant something, they had to. Since they were all in town, it wasn't likely a direct neighbor of any of the girls, but it had to be someone who saw them, coveted something about them. She stood close to the wall, nose an inch from the thumb-tacked map. She stepped back as far as she could, butt pressing against Nick's rickety college desk. She stepped left five paces, changing the angle; she returned to center, then scooted to the right, half her body behind the doorway into the kitchen; those thumbtacks revealed none of their secrets.

She fell onto the couch and put her face in her hands, elbows on her knees. She felt sick. There had to be something, something, something…

She suddenly recalled a brief, though all-encompassing, obsession with New Kids on the Block, back when she was eleven. Her walls were papered with cutouts from teen magazines, posters, and even collector cards. She and three friends had saved up their allowances to buy an entire box of packs—they'd all purchased packs here and there prior—and split things up so that each had a near set and nobody had doubles. She got the New Kids board game for Christmas, playing it over and over with her girlfriends, despite that it wasn't much fun, and when she had no friends around, she forced her little brother, her mother, even her father to play, to listen, to be immersed in New Kids fever. She had a duffle bag, shoes, t-shirts, and sweatbands. She had those first two albums on cassette, as well as every single from their first album.

After that obsession came Milli Vanilli, rocking the New Kids from the block as quickly as they'd come. And after they'd proven to be phonies, she grew weary of pop stars. That scandal being balm on the wound of her parasocial needs. Things were quiet for awhile, but then came Prince, Bowie, Nine Inch Nails—the latter had her mother pulling her aside to talk, studying her wrists and thighs, promising Jaqi that whatever she was going through, that it would pass.

Was the Delson Dollmaker another brightly burning obsession that would disappear?

Did it matter?

The phone rang, startling her from reverie, and she rose from the couch.

"Hello?"

"Is this Jaqi Bazinet?" The voice was manly, the tone was educated.

"Yes? Is this Pierre Allard?"

"Uh huh, what can I do for you?"

Jaqi hadn't quite thought through this essential piece

of the conversation and found herself rambling into a partial truth. "Nick's doing a story on Delson's missing and murdered girls and I'm helping him, since I don't have a job. Nick won't soon either. By next week we'll both be unemployed." She took a deep, noisy breath.

"I can't talk about open cases with civilians; besides, they wouldn't let me near that one." After a moment's pause, Pierre whispered, "I think they suspect my position as a righteous saboteur."

Jaqi was nodding as she listened. "That's okay. What about older cases? Closed ones. And what about cops themselves?"

Pierre did not respond.

"Hello?" Jaqi said.

"Are you doing a story or trying to figure out who the killer is?" Pierre said, his voice still low, though the humor had evaporated. "You know, that would probably make this department look pretty stupid if a college kid figured it out before the detectives."

Jaqi hadn't considered that. "Oh, right o—"

"So, which casefiles do you want to see? I'm trying to see this department look pretty stupid."

This was so unexpected that Jaqi hopped in place. "The murdered and missing girls from the early 'eighties. Eighty-two and eighty-three."

Pierre snorted into laughter. "What are the chances? Somebody's already pulled them. I can't take them out, but if you come by later today, you can look through them. But don't bring a camera with lots of film to take pictures when

I'm called away from the room. Don't you dare do that. Why, that's nearly as bad as stabbing an innocent man like Randy Hyde."

Jaqi was a livewire, thrumming from her scalp to the soles of her feet. "I can come in after lunch. I'll have to—where would a I buy…" she trailed.

"In this town, dependant on budget, I'd go with Black's, which is in the mall next to the Burger King. Can I expect you at, say, one PM?"

The clock on the stove said it was already 11:21 AM. "Yes. One. I'll get there."

"I look forward to seeing you again, Miss Bazinet."

"Yeah, me too, but with you, uh, bye."

Jaqi cradled the receiver and bolted for the bathroom. She needed to shower and dress and buy a camera and some film and… "Aah!"

16

Eugene Longauer sat in the small media room at the front of the police station. He had a tape recorder and a notepad in his lap. To his left was a reporter with a shoulder cam, CBC insignia on his chest. In his hand was a microphone with a red ball, CBC insignia once again, this time splashed around the base to be certain it would always be readable in a shot.

The room's only door opened and both Eugene and the CBC man turned their heads. Instead of someone bringing information, it was a young woman. She had a smaller, newer camera than the CBC reporter. The microphone she withdrew from her bag read: CTV. She looked utterly *new*.

In that moment, Eugene's mind flashed forward ten, fifteen years. There'd always be cops telling reporters their version of events, but how long would print reporters be around? He'd already talked to marcel about the likelihood of the Mirror slipping to a weekly paper with more immediate stories appearing on a website. A couple folks in the breakroom had scoffed, but Eugene did not. The future, for good or bad, was the internet. Then, how long before written news reports were translated from audio, directly into text, then how long until the computers could write the news themselves, then how long before someone exploited the easy come easy go of machine-made products, manipulating the news beyond coloring, then how long until the Canadian government started weaponizing the news? Parts of that bleak future were already in place in other countries, though usually performed in more archaic methods than the digital scope—he'd once watched an investigative report on the quality of information given to the public in places like Russia and Egypt; as expected, citizens in those countries were spoon-fed bullshit, and the only surprising point was that the masses didn't seem to mind all that much.

ATLAS WUNDOR

Before Eugene had too much time to dwell on the notion of numbered days, government information skewing, and human lemmings, the door opened again. Leading the trio of men stepping inside was the Delson chief of police, Robert Thompson. Following Robert was the lead of the six detectives at the station, Adrian Playsic. The third man was not a local, appeared to be a cut above the others. *Neat, tidy, calculated, employed with a different standard*, Eugene thought as he looked the man over from his shiny leather loafers to his tailored blue slacks, to his creamy white button-up, complete with a blue silk tie, silver tie slide, and crisp, perfectly measured collar. His face was bland, clean-shaven; his hair was a little longer than a crew cut and sat uniformly on his ovular head. Robert had always been a bit of a joke, but next to this new guy, the punchline of the joke became cringey. Adrien, in his defense, had spent years looking up the company ladder to see a slob, so his attire and how he carried himself were kept to a low, low bar.

"All right. Let's get this moving. No questions until I'm through," Robert said from behind a podium with the Delson PD crest mounted on its face. "We're here to update and confirm some things. To begin, we have yet to receive any note or call concerning the whereabouts of Melissa Sparks. It is possible the person who abducted and murdered the young women last summer, and up until recently, is the same individual responsible for taking Ms. Sparks.

"Most of the details, and why we can publicly state

that we think it's the same person, must remain confidential. We've been overwhelmed with bogus confessions; making certain pieces of information vital. Now, that said, we have no suspects at this time, though we do have many persons of interest. We're asking the public to remain diligent, lock your doors, and mind your daughters. It is very unlikely this individual will suddenly take an interest in a different age group or gender.

"Finally, before we get to questions, the RCMP has sent us a detective here from Ottawa. Detective Rejean Leibert will be with us, hopefully, until we catch this guy. Did you want to say anything?" Robert leaned forward over the podium to look to the man. Rejean shook his head gently. "All right, let's have the questions."

The young woman from CTV did not wait on further invitation and held out her mic, putting it in the visual frame of her camera lens. "Detective Leibert."

Looking annoyed, he stepped to the podium. "Yes?"

"I take it you've been around many police stations. Is Delson simply especially bad, letting all these women be taken so easily?"

Rejean snorted and waved a hand at the woman, as if shooing her away.

"Have you caught a serial killer before?" the CBC reporter asked.

"No," Rejan said. "They aren't common. I have been part of two teams that caught serial rapists, however. The crime here is undoubtedly more severe, but the method of capture will be the same."

"You think you'll catch him?" CTV asked.

"Nearly all active criminals face the music eventually," Rejean said.

Eugene cleared his throat. "What's being done on the law end to prevent further abductions? And what did you learn from Charlaine Chabot's remains?"

Rejean gave a half grin and stepped back from the podium. Robert returned and said, "We're encouraging the public to remain vigilant. We're patrolling regularly, which now includes officers pulling overtime. As for Charlaine Chabot: as noted previously, she'd recently given birth, and the timeline suggests the pregnancy was the outcome of an assault. We also know whoever took her has space, privacy, and patience. We're not prepared to divulge further."

"What makes a person a person of interest in this case?" CTV asked.

Robert sighed. "Age, gender, location, resources, and abilities."

"What age?" CBC asked.

Robert shifted his bulk further onto the podium. "We're thinking it's a man between twenty and sixty."

Eugene whistled, then asked, "How many persons of interest are on your list?"

Robert shook his head gently. "Next question."

"Will you step down if you don't catch him?' CTV asked.

Robert straightened up, deep, angry wrinkles casting shadows about his pudgy face. "What kind of question is that?" He took a step toward the door. "Press conference over."

The CBC reporter and Eugene turned to the CTV reporter to give her a look. It was important to get enough stuff to fill out a story before asking questions that might blow a man's fuse.

"My rule," CBC said, "is to ask questions for five minutes before I try a gotcha…if I ever bother. You'll be lucky if he speaks in front of you again."

The young woman set the microphone down on the chair currently holding her camera. Her eyebrows went up as she shifted her weight to her left hip. "He has to speak in front of me. I'm the media. The public has a right to know what's happening."

"Yeah, and they can get it from me," CBC said.

Eugene huffed an aggravated breath. "The public has no right to know much of anything. Not everyone even has the right to eat food or drink water. Thompson's not a forgiving sort, you've probably screwed your station out of footage."

"He can't ban me from the news," CTV said, though all certainty she'd harbored in her tone prior had now evaporated.

CBC finished packing his camera and mic into a padded canvas bag. "You want my advice? Cut and dye your hair, put on glasses, get some heels, and maybe show some cleavage. Good cleavage can distract the hell out of an angry man."

"That's sexist," CTV said.

"Maybe, but there've been times in my career where I wish I had a fine rack, hell, any rack. Sexism is just sex from a less than agreeable vantage point, that doesn't mean it can't exist in the public and be manipulated for personal gain," CBC said.

Eugene was on his feet heading to the door, grinning. While what the man from the CBC had said sucked, it was typically a fact, and a recent grad's ideals weren't going to change it an iota. Not anytime soon.

"See y'all around," Eugene said, stepping out into the station's foyer.

17

Nick decided to eat his lunch with the musty newspapers in the dank basement rather than joining the rest of the Mirror staff in the breakroom. He was beginning to feel at odds with all of them, not just the ones who gave reason. Besides, he needed to remain focussed on his real task. He'd reached 1983—in a reading sense; impossible to have the scanning keep pace. He read of finding the bodies of the girls who'd gone missing in 1982. He read about Josie Boschman, a fifteen-year-old who'd been taken in late evening, sometime after her shift ended at King Cheese Pizza. He read of Shawnie Gosselin who was taken from her home, and when her parents returned from a night out, they discovered the shower still running and the back door forced open. He read of the arrest of Donny Tiffany, read of the confession, read of the commendations the mayor and then the premier of the province gave Robert Thompson. He read of the cops locating the remains of Josie and Shawnie, then of the abduction and murder of Marcy Beareau. Unlike what the old man had suggested, this one did seem quite different: though she was taken from her home, on a night her family was away, and the back door was forced open; she was sexually assaulted and dumped shortly thereafter. Her entire absence lasted less than a week.

Nick reached August. He skimmed pages and nearly passed by another missing young woman. Doreen Barber was taken from her home on August 29th, 1983. Apparently, since it *couldn't* be related to the others, Marcel—prior to becoming editor of the Mirror—scored details pertaining to the scene in a way that hadn't occurred with previous abductees.

"Holy shit," he whispered; assuming they'd railroaded Donny Tiffany—Nick was really starting to buy in that they had—a fourth victim, and maybe… "Holy shit, what if there's more?"

The story was more like a profile on the girl than a crime report. But there, in the fourth paragraph, Marcel got into the crime. Doreen was fourteen and her parents had both been on the night shift at the casket plant all week. Doreen was babysitting her little sister and brother, but both children went to bed knowing their sister was in the living room watching TV, and neither heard a peep in the night. At some point between 9:30 PM and 5:50 AM, someone cut a hole through a basement window, slipped into the home unnoticed, and left with Doreen. There were minor signs of struggle in the living room, but nothing to suggest Doreen accomplished much in a fight.

"Didn't break the window, he cut it," Nick said, thinking, *Certainly would be quieter…cut glass?*

The image of a rugged, old-timey piece of molded plastic came to mind. It had steel ends, one being rectangular with a reinforced corner and gaps cut along the bottom something like jack-o-lantern teeth. The other end was a weighty ball for tapping the cut glass free. His grandmother jumped from one discipline to another without making much art, though she always had supplies ready and waiting. She'd told Nick he could keep the cutter as long as he made something for her with it. The first time he used it was on a discarded windowpane; he cut his hands badly enough that he didn't return to it, even after his mother encouraged him to push through the pain—a few cuts would never kill him…just don't bleed on the carpet.

Briefly, he wondered what had become of the thing, then shoved it from his mind. He needed to find out what happened to Doreen. He flipped and flipped and flipped. He pulled the 1985 book from the shelf, then the 1986 book. None mentioned Doreen Barber.

"Huh," he said, and got back to scanning.

18

Melissa refused to open her eyes after awakening to rumblings beyond the walls of the little room, bedding clutched in a white-knuckled grip.

"Go back to sleep," she whispered, trying to push herself back just a minute or two, slip into elsewhere. "Sleep."

She'd dreamt of running on an empty street, bolting up the driveway home, and finding her mother in the kitchen making the heart-shaped pancakes she made when Melissa was a little girl. Now, far too awake for comfort, the sudden thrust into reality was enough to spark fresh tears.

Click.

The slot midway down the door had opened. She felt the slim atmospheric change, felt the man's presence even if he remained all but out of sight. "Come now," said the voice, through the serving slot. "You'll be home sooner than later, if you behave. Good girls behave."

He'd come into her room—prison—last night. He wore the ski mask he had when he'd taken her and nothing else. Melissa had seen penises before, but they'd always been erect. The flaccid little toadstool in that patch of black fur—a few grey strands had invaded the mat—was so much worse for the dutiful ease the man felt about himself. In his hand was a syringe, which he promised would make her stay easier. She didn't dare fight when he pressed the needle's tip to a vein inside her elbow; the punches she'd taken already left her petrified...that they could come so quickly and leave such lingering pain made her want to scream for mercy, beg the man, do anything and everything he ordered, but now, if she could keep hold of the dream, then maybe, maybe, maybe...

"Do you want me to come in there?"

That opened her eyes. He'd left not long after stripping her drugged body—his penis hadn't stiffened until he started on her makeup. The rape had taken minutes, or hours, or days, or maybe just seconds.

Now, Melissa was still naked beneath her blanket, a little groggy from that shot. "I'm awake," she whispered, eying the trey sitting on the slot's platform.

She held the blanket up to her neck as she crawled to the end of the bed. He'd seen her naked, obviously, but every moment he saw her, every moment she considered his leering gaze, it made her flesh roil in miniature, though violent, trembles. She was disgusted, she was confused, she was as ashamed of herself as she'd ever been.

"Why me?" she said, reaching for the trey with one hand while holding the blanket with the other.

"You've grown into such a beautiful young woman; why would it be anybody but you? Now, eat."

The slot flipped closed with a clank, and Melissa studied the offering: a small pile of walnuts, nine cherry tomatoes, two clementines, a container of full-fat yogurt, a tin of sardines, and a sleeve of saltines. On its side was a bottle of spring water. Beneath a spoon was a sample-size pack of Mary Kay makeup wipes. She picked up the spoon and caught her reflection: lipstick streaking her cheek, mascara raccooning her eyes.

—

Melissa sat on the toilet bucket reading one of the books not based on pregnancy. This one, instead, was about an intricate murder plot that placed blame on a detective named Lam. She'd heard of Erle Stanley Gardner, but didn't know from where. Typically, she didn't much go for mysteries, but this one helped pass agonizing time thanks to an especially heavy period. She'd known it was coming—had spotted yesterday—but hadn't quite connected that her abductor would want the information, perhaps have supplies prepared.

Eventually, the slot opened with a meal of roast beef, mashed potatoes, and a bottle of 2% milk. "Come."

"I can't." Her voice was sheepish, and she knew then, if she got the chance to escape, she wouldn't dare in case he caught her. How bad would it be if he caught her? How much worse?

"Do you want me to come in there?"

"It's my…I need tampons or pads…I'm—"

The man made a disgusted scoffing sound. "That's one; you only get two more."

"What?" she said, but no response came for several seconds. When the Kotex box appeared next to her supper, she said, "Thank you."

Toilet paper held in place, she shuffled to the door. The meal went to the cot and she returned to the bucket. As she inserted a tampon, her eyes fell to the single bloody dot on the grey cement floor. With two squares of toilet paper folded over, she bent forward. As she wiped At the blood that had already begun to seep into the concrete, she dared a glance to those dark eye sockets sunken into that leathery face beneath her cot. That body celled off in the wall.

"I don't want to be you. What do I do?" she whispered.

The mummified corpse did not reply.

"Please?"

Again, no reply came.

Melissa climbed onto the cot, sobbing, thinking of her mother's cooking once more as she shoveled the surprisingly decent, albeit cool, food into her mouth. The scent from the bucket was enough to sour even a modicum of dignity she found in the offering.

19

Jaqi ran across the parking lot, passing two uniformed cops who gave her sideways looks. She offered both a minor, forced smile to convey there was no emergency beyond her slight lateness. Hopefully, that lateness wouldn't sour Pierre Allard. From experience, she knew many middle-aged men were inordinately offended when deciding they'd been wronged by a woman, forget a young woman.

But her lateness wasn't her fault, not exactly.

On her way to Black's, she'd had a minor epiphany that what they had in stock wasn't exactly what she needed—at least not within a mediocre budget. While her father's money was available to her, there was no reason to make any purchases big enough to garner an unscheduled call.

The man behind the counter at Delson Pawn had convinced her to shift the epiphanous idea of what she needed, meaning she'd still go over the budget she'd set initially, but maybe she'd make a record of every report and piece collected as evidence. Every single piece.

"I'm here…" Jaqi huffed a deep breath, "to see…Officer Allard."

"You a Miss Bazinet?" The woman running the intake window was highly unenthusiastic.

"Yes."

The woman reached to her left, hit a button, and the door into the bullpen buzzed as it unlatched. Jaqi moved quickly, as if these few seconds would make a difference when she was already behind the clock.

"He's waiting for you in room one." The woman pointed across the busy space and its many cubicles to a door clearly marked INTERROGATION #1. "Try not to stab anyone on your way back."

A few laughs sounded from within the bullpen as Jaqi shuffled along, knocking once before opening the door a crack to lean her face inside. "Officer Allard?"

Pierre Allard was on the floor doing push-ups. "Oh, there you are. You're late." Pierre popped to his feet and brushed his hands together.

Jaqi stepped into the room. On the floor and table were more than a dozen bankers' boxes. The room smelled like cigarettes and dust. The drop ceiling was yellowed from smoke with brown swatches, assumedly from a leaky pipe. The amount of stuff was staggering, but her plan remained firm.

"Sorry, I went to Black's and—"

"Shht. Geez, can't much have a conversation without coffee. Guess I'll have to go to Tim Hortons for us." Pierre looked at a gold wristwatch. "I'll be back in forty-one minutes. You don't mind watching this stuff until I get back?"

Pierre wore no readable expression and Jaqi wondered if there were cameras and microphones somewhere. "I, uh, is someone watching me?"

"No. Not listening, either." Pierre smiled. "See you soon. At about two, get me?"

"Yes," Jaqi said, already reaching into her crammed-full purse.

"Lock the door behind me," Pierre said as he passed her.

Once he was gone, Jaqi spun the little peak on the

inside of the doorknob. This was nothing more than a warning lock. She probably couldn't get into much trouble herself, but if they were looking to get rid of Pierre—which it sounded as if they shouldn't mind an excuse to do so—she didn't want to give anyone the necessary fuel to pull that particular trigger. He seemed like a sweet one in a town that was straight sour.

She slipped the mini camcorder she'd purchased at Dave's Pawn from her purse. She plugged the charger into the wall. At the table, she recorded the label from the end of the box, the marker faded but plenty legible. Lid popped off, she withdrew the first folder. Tricky, she held the camcorder in one hand and flipped the pages slowly. After the first five, she hit STOP, then REWIND. She watched the footage in the device's tiny display window and could only hope for the best when it was blown up onto a TV screen.

She shot footage of every page from every box. She shot footage of pictures, pieces of evidence from brown paper bags. She shot footage of the bags themselves. Less than a minute after she flopped onto one of the room's three chairs, sweaty and exhausted and totally stressed, a knock played against the door.

"Is someone in there?" a voice said.

Jaqi launched to her feet, stashing the camcorder in her bag as she broke for the door. She turned the little lock handle and pulled open the door a crack. "Yes?"

"Who are you?" asked a cross-eyed cop in full uniform.

"I'm Jaqi Bazinet. Officer Allard put me in here. He wants to ask me some questions."

"About what?"

Before Jaqi could muster a convincing lie, Pierre's voice carried toward her and the cross-eyed cop. "She's helping me identify a serial jaywalker."

The cross-eyed cop made an expression of disgust. "Fucking whatever, buddy. Fucking asshole." He stepped back into the bullpen, stopping at a desk where a teenaged boy with a tear-smeary face sat in wait, hands cuffed behind his back.

"Get what you needed?"

"I hope so."

Pierre nodded. "Better run along while I put those boxes back the way they were. Don't be a stranger now, you hear?" He winked.

"I won't," Jaqi said feeling wrung out.

—

Jaqi plugged the RCA cords into the front of Nick's DVD/VCR player, closed her eyes, and said a little prayer to the universe: "Please, please, please work." She took three deep breaths, then hit PLAY on the camcorder.

The screen of the 32" Toshiba went from grey fuzz to the image of a box. The words on the side were legible: SHAWNIE GOSSELIN #2. Her heart was racing; at no time while recording did she doubt she'd be able to read the large handwriting on the boxes. She watched herself dig free a folder. Jaqi swallowed, hands balled into fists, knowing it was stupid not to have just bought a camera and heaps of film, that this little bit of corner cutting would—

Jaqi leapt up like she'd just made out with Molly Ringwald after being let free from weekend detention, right fist raised high. "Yeeeaaah!" she shouted, deep and throaty. The writing on the screen wasn't crisp, but it was legible. She hit pause and a few fuzz lines appeared here and there, but hardly marred the quality.

Jaqi melted into the couch, so relieved she hadn't wasted her chance. The urge to call Nick, the urge to call Pierre, the urge to tell someone how well her scheme worked was nearly strong enough to set her in motion. Instead, she settled herself down and started reading, note pad before her on the coffee table. This information did little good if she didn't comb through it.

After reaching the halfway point of a page of notes, she rewound the little cassette in the camcorder and found the setting that would show the time stamp on the screen. She put the origin time next to each of the bullet points she'd written so far. The pen danced. The images on the screen froze and unfroze, freezing again almost immediately. The pen danced anew. She kept it up for hours, unnoticing of a sore back, dry eyes, and a very hungry tummy until Nick stepped through the door.

"There was another girl," Nick said, and at the same time Jaqi said, "That cop let me record case files."

"What?" Nick said just as Jaqi said, "What?"

20

"Who's this?" Zach said as he climbed from his truck, pulling into his driveway next to Kris' work truck.

Kris and a small man with slim shoulders, thin arms, about 1% body fat, and long brown hair had been sitting on the tailgate of Kris' truck. Each had a bottle of Busch beer in hand.

"This is my cousin, Pete," Kris said.

Zach approached with his hand out, though harbored a concerned and confused expression. This Pete guy wasn't the typical sort Kris palled around with.

Pete took the offered shake and traded it for a limp noodle grip. "Howdy."

"Right," Zach said. "What's up?"

"I know how we'll get him," Kris said. His eyes were intense, his mouth twisted into an angry, though smiling sneer. I know just how we'll catch this motherfucker."

"How?" Zach said.

Kris pointed at Pete. Pete made kissy lips.

"What the fuck are you talking about?" Zach said, just about ready to take extreme offense to this frilly little dude pulling faces at him.

"Pete's going to dress up and act like a chick." Kris said this as if it should be obvious.

Zach shook his head in tight, angry strokes. "What?"

"It'll be the perfect bait and switch. My daughter Pauline's fourteen and she has fucking high school seniors nosing around."

"Okay? You want to get your daughter—"

Kris waved a hand. "No, no. What we'll do is have her sunbathe out front of the house a bunch. She's obsessed with getting a tan and her mother's trying to keep her pale. I think she's hoping Pauline won't get up to much if she's not looking brown, or something. So, Pauline don't even need to know any of the plan; she's already all for tanning on the front yard and she's pissed enough at her mom to come by after school to do it without yapping about it. It's perfect."

Zach twisted his mouth to the left side of his face as he squinted. "I don't get it."

"Just think about it a bit, why don't you," Pete said, tone utterly saucy.

"Pete, please," Kris said. "See, during the day, Pauline is going to sit around getting attention, and every night, it's going to be Pete with me in the house. Pete fits almost perfectly into Pauline's clothes."

"'Cept I don't have any tits or ass."

"You can stuff," Kris said to Pete, then turned back to Zach. "He don't even mind dressing like a chick. He's queer as a fucking three-dollar-bill. Ever since he come back from Kingston."

"Kingston Pen?"

Kris nodded.

Zach was adding it together and he'd heard of worse

plans. Plenty of them. "What were you in Kingston for?"

"Grand theft auto, possession of cocaine, intent to sell cocaine, and assaulting a police officer." Pete said this as if it bored him. "And, for the record, I was queer long before I went in, just didn't know it."

"Okay, right, okay," Zach said. "Then what, do we all have to wait at your house, or you going to call the cops when the guy shows up?"

"We can take turns if everybody can't be there every night. I'll have to make a show of leaving for the bar; the guy always knows when the girl's home alone."

Zach leaned his back against one of the rear fenders of Kris' truck and inhaled deeply through his nose. Spring was on the air; one of his neighbors was mowing their lawn and another was planting flowers. The fresh cut grass scent was nice—whether the flower scent was strong enough to add, it was impossible to know—and might've even helped Zach decide if he wanted to be part of this particular scheme.

"Yeah, all right. Guess we run it past the guys tonight?" Zach said.

Kris clapped his hands together once. "Right on. I'll bring Pete around tonight—"

"What if the guy's already been watching your daughter? What if he shows up tonight?"

Kris waved once more. "She's sleeping at her mom's. Guess if someone shows up tonight, they'll do so at an empty house."

"Or, instead of going to The Bruce, we just meet up

at your place. Save a few bucks on beer?"

Summer was supposed to be his time to really rake in some dough, squirrel it away for the slow days of winter. Catching this fuck was important, but so was keeping his house.

21

Nick had been home about two minutes, long enough to make a visit to the toilet, grab a glass of juice, and settle in next to Jaqi on the couch. The living room was an organized mess of paper, and Nick was adding to it.

"So, who was she?" Jaqi asked.

Just about any other day, this question would put a man on guard, but Nick didn't even look away from the pages. Nick had a file folder in his grip and held it up like a stop sign.

"Doreen Barber was treated as a runaway, but everything matches with the others, *and* with what's happening lately and last year—at least that's how it looks in the papers."

Jaqi snatched the chunky folder and began flipping through the copies of the old articles. She skimmed until finding the unenthusiastic offering concerning the girl's disappearance, then gasped when she reached about the halfway point, reached the bit about cut glass. The rest of the folder slipped from her hands, and she waved the single page at Nick.

"They kept the bit about glass from the media, remember? It's him! He's doing it again! That guy's innocent!"

Nick made a *calm down* gesture with his hands. "Okay, cool out. You'll get us evicted. You're saying the entry method was the same and they still...Jesus Christ." Nick rubbed his jaw, a slight five o'clock shadow sandpapering his palm. "Okay, this is big. We need to plan. We need to build up evidence...fucking huge. Donny Tiffany has been in prison for like thirteen years."

"Thirteen years," Jaqi said as she bent to collect the mess of pages she'd made, her enthusiasm drained. "What kind of lawyer could a guy like this get?"

Nick stepped into the kitchen and swung open the fridge door. He grabbed two bottles of Moosehead and waved for Jaqi to follow him. "Public defender. Come on. I need a smoke." Once onto the balcony, he showed Jaqi his stained hands. "I scrubbed them. Going to look like frostbite by the end of the week."

Jaqi wasn't listening, her gaze vacantly playing over the distant horizon of buildings. "If we nail this down tight." She shook her head. "If we do it perfect, or close to, it's going to be so much bigger than just you getting another job."

"Yeah, I was thinking there's enough for a book," Nick said.

Jaqi let out a monosyllabic huff of laughter. "Book, I guess, but we could save a man's life. Maybe save a girl's life! Mandy Sparks—"

"Melissa."

"Right! Melissa Sparks! She's out there, and so is a killer, and some useless cop is running the fucking investigation!"

After swallowing a mouthful of cold beer, he twisted the cap from Jaqi's bottle and handed it to her. "Take a sip and cool it with the yelling."

Jaqi seemed to come to then, blinking at Nick. "You're right, sorry. I'm…this is big. Bigger than getting a Master's in physical therapy."

Nick stiffened. "What?"

Bottle to her lips, Jaqi spoke before drinking: "Don't worry, I'm not dropping out or something. It's just, this is big." She drank, swallowed. "This is bigger than big." She put down her bottle and wrapped her arms around Nick's neck, pressing her body to his.

"Very big."

"Big?" Jaqi said as she ground her upper thigh into the crotch of his jeans. "How big."

Nick tossed his cigarette into the coffee can in the corner. "Getting bigger by the second," he whispered, slowly thrusting into her motions.

Six minutes later, Nick returned to his beer. Jaqi was leaned over the railing, momentarily spent.

"Want a smoke?" he said.

Sometimes she did, after sex or when she was drinking.

"I will," she said, shuffling inside with her pants and underwear bunched beneath her ass.

Nick lit a fresh dart from his pack, then pulled the sliding door closed.

22

The Brown trailer sat at the rear of the park. The backyard was twelve feet from the ten-foot fence that blocked off a modicum of the sounds and smells that blew in from the chicken barns a quarter mile away. Stacy-Lynn Brown's parents had gone into town for Bingo at the Legion—as they did every week.

Stacy-Lynn had her eyes on the clock. It was after nine and Mikey Keane was overdue—her parents wouldn't be home until at least eleven. She'd started working the till afterschool at McDonald's; Mikey worked in the back. The nine-year age difference thrilled Stacy-Lynn, perhaps because she knew none of the adults in her life would approve—not that her father wasn't twelve years older than her mother, her mother who'd given birth to Stacy-Lynn when she was seventeen. Stacy-Lynn would be sixteen in a few weeks; she was plain, her bodily features were muted, her flesh was marred by fresh acne and scars from ancient acne, she took general classes at school and only scraped by, and she had an undeserving rep because she'd given a popular twelve-grader a blowjob one night at a party the summer before starting high school.

But Mikey, he was different. He didn't mind any of her faults, he had a licence—and his mom's car whenever she wasn't using it—and was old enough to ply her and her friends with sugary rum coolers. They hadn't gone all the way, but she was ready, and it was inevitable. Even her mother saw that truth, and rather than fighting the fact, she built up her daughter's defenses.

"'You ain't gonna end up like me,'" she said, quoting her mother in a whiny, nasally tone as she rubbed a needle bump bulging from her forearm. Her eyes fell back to the clock. "Come on."

She scooped her phone from the receiver and was about to dial when she heard something from the back of the trailer. She killed the TV with the remote. A smile lit her face. Mikey was trying to scare her.

After flicking off the hall light, she walked on tippy toes, into a darkness she knew like it was part of her person. Something pinged and the window slid open audibly. Stacy-Lynn leaned against the hallway wall, hands to her mouth to stifle the sound of laughter. A boy who'd go to these lengths for a fun little prank would— *but the windows are locked; Dad put locks on the windows because he's terrified of...*

With a shaking hand, Stacy-Lynn flicked another light switch. The trailer revealed itself, revealed the shadowy doorway of her parents' bedroom.

"Mikey?" Stacy-Lynn said taking a step closer.

For a heartbeat it was as if the shadow had come to life. A man in head-to-toe black poured from the room, arms out, reaching for Stacy-Lynn. She swung at those horrid hands, but they were strong, determined, and skilled. They encircled her throat; instantly the pressure built and it felt as if her eyes would pop. And the burn, all over the burn. She sucked and gasped, her arms flailing as she clawed at the man's gloved hands.

—

"Tell me you're not going out to screw that little high school chick," Ronald said. "That shit, man, it ain't worth it."

"Man, she's eighteen. She just got held back a couple times. Nobody'd lie about that," Mikey Keane said as he slipped his feet into his sneakers.

After work, he'd gone home for a quick shower, then went out to play video games with the guys. Tonight, it was only Ronald and his cousin Jonny, who'd moved in less than a week ago.

"Dude, chicks do nothing but lie," Jonny said.

"Bros before hos," Ronald said.

"Money over bitches," Jonny said.

"Bitches ain't shit but hos and tricks," Ronald said.

"Yeah, but it ain't no fun if your homie don't get none," Mikey said, standing and fishing a couple four-packs of Bacardi coolers that tasted like Creamsicle from the fridge.

"Be careful, for real. Get her to show you some ID. Prison ain't no joke, man," Ronald said, finally peeling his eyes from the TV screen and *NHL '97*. "Seriously."

"Only thing you got going when you find out she's a little kid is that she's trailer trash and no cop's gonna give a fuck if she's fucking," Jonny said, squinting and tilting his body, as if it might make the little Saku Koivu on screen move faster, make the little Pierre Turgeon wheel smoother, make the goddamned Jocelyn Thibault stop the puck now and then—the score was currently 9-3 for Ronald's Avalanche over Jonny's Canadiens.

Ronald's digital Joe Sakic skated from the boards, through the hashmarks in front of Jonny's Jocelyn Thibault, and fired an unstoppable shot.

"No fucking EA goals!" Jonny shouted.

Ronald cackled, laughing.

Mikey left, grinning. He hadn't been laid in more than a year and tonight would be the night; Stacy-Lynn had all but promised as much.

—

"What's that from?" a man said through a door slot.

Stacy-Lynn attempted to sit up. She was on a cot, in an unfamiliar room. Her head was ringing and she ached deep into her bones. The taste of blood was heavy on her tongue. "What?" she said, the word crackly as a blown speaker.

"You have a needle mark."

Stacy-Lynn put a hand to her shoulder, finger prodding the lump at the center of a swollen mound of flesh. "Where am I?"

"What's it from?"

"Are you him?" Stacy-Lynn said through budding tears. "Are you going to rape me and kill me?"

"Hush, nothing like that. What's the shot from?"

"It's…it's Depo-Provera. It's so I don't get pregnant, like my mom did."

The man sighed.

"Please, I'm…please, don't hurt me."

"Be right back. You sound thirsty."

Stacy-Lynn looked around the little room, reality setting in more and more fully with each passing moment. She kicked from the cot and tried the door handle. Locked. She banged. Heavy steel. She tried the paneling—she'd helped her dad with a weekend reno job once; he'd easily Kool-Aid Manned himself through a paneled wall, which had everyone in attendance rolling with laughter. She slammed the backs of her hands against the soft, shiny wood. The report was dull, ungiving. She grabbed the cot and shook it, feeling for something she might turn into a weapon. The cot was WWIII solid, ready for an apocalypse survivor's back and bolted to the floor. She dropped to her knees, and gasped.

There was a tiny cell inset into the wall. Inside was a body of some form, facing away. The hair was dark and scraggly. An ankle was visible below the hem of a light blue dress. It had gone brown, dehydrated, mummified. Stacy-Lynn swallowed.

Behind her, the man's voice said, "Here, have a drink.

Don't worry about her."

"Who is it?" Stacy-Lynn said, mind flipping. She needed a plan if she couldn't bludgeon this guy.

"Never mind. I brought you a Coke."

Stacy-Lynn rose and accepted the plastic bottle. It was sealed, the little teeth between the cap and the ring that existed below the rim's hump was intact. She was so thirsty, so damned thirsty. She cracked the lid. The pop hissed and danced from the mouth in minute explosions. She dipped her tongue. It tasted like Coca-Cola.

"I didn't do anything to it," the man said.

Stacy-Lynn did not trust him, but the bottle looked perfect and tasted fine. She tipped it back and drank it down below the top edge of the red label. She took a deep breath, then went in for another helping. It was more than half-gone before she felt a swimmy wave wash over her mind. She capped the bottle; pop was running up her arm. She blinked, stumbling backward until her legs hit the cot and sent her down.

"What?" she said.

She turned over the capped bottle. There was a tiny puncture wound that wept slowly from the center of the rough circle left by the machine that manufactured the bottle. She blinked, everything fuzzy. She was high. The door opened and the man stepped into the little room. He had no mask on.

Sleepily, Stacy-Lynn looked at her captor and said, "Oh, it's you?"

23

Nick heard a sound coming from beyond the bedroom. He touched Jaqi's side of the bed, finding it empty and cool. Gentle light played around the mostly closed door. The clock read: 4:58.

He kicked his legs free of their sheets and stood. Arms above his head, on tippy toes, he stretched his spine. He walked stiffly, eyes squinted against the living room light. Jaqi stood in shorts and a threadbare halter top, looking at the wall of maps and Post-it notes they'd stuck up so far.

"Can't sleep?" Nick said.

"Do you think Charlaine Chabot's baby is still alive? The one she had while kidnapped."

Nick wrapped his arms around Jaqi's shoulders from behind, putting his face next to her left ear. "Maybe. I don't know."

"What would a man, and maybe a woman, too, do with a newborn?" Jaqi said.

"I don't know." Nick kissed her ear. "Maybe it was stillborn."

Jaqi leaned her head away from Nick. "Your breath… Did you ever hear of a serial killer called Albert Fish?"

Nick let go of Jaqi and dropped down onto the couch.

"Don't think so."

"There was this girl name Marilynn in my sixth-grade class. She was on some kind of missionary trade; her mother came to class every day with her, too. She was from Papua New Guinea, and she was weird. She never mentioned God or Satan or anything, but everything was good or evil, the middle didn't exist. Anyway, the teacher had a weird obsession with the girl and told us to give an oral report of someone good or evil from history."

Nick sat rubbing his eyes, mostly listening, but also on the cusp of tipping off, heading back into dreamland on the next express train.

"I don't remember who I did mine on, but Marilynn did her report on Albert Fish. He killed and ate children, not babies, but children. After it was done, he sent a letter to the mother of one of the little girls he killed, which the cops tracked down because of the letterhead or something. The Dollmaker doesn't do any of that extra stuff."

Nick yawned, eyes now fully closed. "And?"

"Fish obviously wanted to be caught, or at minimum wanted to flaunt what he'd done. How do you figure out who's the bad guy when he doesn't want to be caught?"

"Call it profiling, I think," Nick said, the words soft around the edges.

"So, what's this guy's profile?" When Nick didn't answer, Jaqi spun and charged at the couch. She put her hands on Nick's shoulders and shook. "Come on! What do we know about him?"

Nick opened his eyes wide. "Shit. Geez. I don't know.

He likes girls and does their makeup before or after he rapes and murders them?"

"Okay, but what else? We know he has a lot of privacy."

Nick waved at this. "So does everybody more than a mile out of town."

"Not like the Dollmaker. Think. Charlaine Chabot was kept long enough to get pregnant and then have the child. That takes at least a big house or shed. I mean, the guy has to play normal during the day, or he wouldn't have so much information. He wouldn't even know who to grab!"

Nick sat up with a huff. "We're getting loud, and it's early."

"So what?" Jaqi said, shaking him again.

"Quit. Stop." Nick frowned at his girlfriend—he had to be at work in a few hours and she could take as many catnaps as she liked through the day.

"What do we know?" she said, sitting down and leaning her head against Nick's shoulder.

"Okay. We know he has space and privacy. We know he's local. We know he can hang around without being noticed, or possibly his partner could do that part. We know he knows how to put on make up. We know he sexually assaults the girls. We know one gave birth to his child. We know he was active in the early 'eighties and quit until last summer."

Jaqi nodded against his bare forearm. "So, what happened to trigger his actions?"

"I don't know."

"I think it has to do with a woman. I was reading some of the notes I copied, and a cop had mused over how killers often have mommy issues. There's nothing to prove this, but what if the guy's mother died and he lost it, started killing, then something happened to stop the cycle until it could start up afresh? I could be misremembering, but I think Albert Fish's mother died right before he did what he did."

Nick looked at Jaqi. "Really? Mommy issues, is that true?"

Jaqi could only shrug.

It was a window and he took the opportunity on offer. "I need at least another hour and a half. See you soon."

Jaqi did not protest, nor did she follow him back to bed. By the time he reached their bedroom door, Jaqi was again standing before the wall of evidence, piecing the story together.

24

Jonny Adams awoke to a fist in his guts and a fat cop in a bulletproof vest looming over the couch where he'd been sleeping. Another big cop was pushing a bloody-faced Ronald Adams, in only boxer shorts, toward the apartment's door. Two more cops were rooting through closets and drawers. These men were too many and too big for such a small space. The bong on the coffee table wasn't adding to the vibe, either.

"What the—" Jonny said, hands up to block any shots aimed for his face.

"Where the fuck's the girl, scumbag?" The fat cop gave Jonny another punch to the gut.

Jonny balled as small as he could without leaving the comforting nature of the couch. "What girl? What fucking girl?" he shouted from behind his arms.

—

Mikey Keane had arrived at Stacy-Lynn Brown's trailer about an hour after she'd been abducted. The front door was locked, and so, thinking it might be a fun joke, he went to the back door of the trailer, though found it locked as well.

"Real safe," he mumbled when he spotted the open window.

He climbed into the empty family home and snuck his way through the house, looking for Stacy-Lynn. She'd ditched him.

"Little bitch," he said and decided he'd wait a while, in case something had come up.

From the fridge he selected a bottle of Labatt's Blue and twisted away the cap. He dropped onto the ancient, sunken couch and began flipping through the basic cable offerings. He drank two beers and passed nine times through the stations before giving up; the little bitch had indeed ditched him.

He went to Stacy-Lynn's room, unzipped, and stroked himself onto her pillow. That would teach her for standing him up. It was after two o'clock when he started out of the quiet trailer park and headed for home, unaware that he'd been observed and identified by one of Stacy-Lynn's neighbors.

A car was sent in his direction. Along the way, an APB filled the airwaves over the radio: the body of a girl was discovered in Kingsman Park and Mikey Keane was wanted for questioning.

"Get the fuck off me!" Mikey Keane screamed as a knee dug into his spine. He only stopped screaming when that knee pressed into the back of his neck and suddenly oxygen was a rare commodity.

25

All was normal, by new standards anyway, when Nick got into the Mirror's office. He nodded to Marcel on the way by, threw a wave to Eugene, and avoided eye contact with the ready-to-burst Martine on his way to the basement. Overlarge travel mug by his side, he continued on with 1983. By the time he reached November in scanning, he had already decided he was going to jump forward to last summer.

One day scanning was fine, dirty but fine. Today sucked, though, and he could only imagine tomorrow and so on. It would get worse and worse every hour he was in this dank basement. He needed to get onto the important point of his task because it seemed highly unlikely that he'd get up to much of anything after today.

"Fuck 'em," he whispered, thinking, let them come down and screw around in this damp, monotonous pit they call a basement.

A great ruckus rang out above him a few minutes after 10:00 AM. Curious, Nick brushed his hands on his pantlegs, grabbed his travel mug for a refill from the pot in the breakroom, and started for the slim set of steps up to the real world. One thing about the basement, damp, smelly, and dark as it was, the temperature was wonderfully cool, no matter how hot it got in the main office. With printers going and blowhards blowing, it didn't take long for the mercury to dance upward in any newsroom.

With each step, the air grew warmer, dryer, and less smelly; it also grew louder. The basement door lined up perfectly with the front door at the far end of a long hallway. On either side were offices, at the front was the sales bullpen of ceiling-less, three-walled cubicles.

"What's going on?" he said, barely catching Eugene and Martine slipping out the front door. "Where is everybody?"

Erica Bellerose was in the breakroom and popped her

head out. "Martine went into labor and the cops made an arrest after another body turned up! Where have you been?"

"In the basement?"

Erica huffed and shook her head as she hurried toward the front with her purse in hand. She had the gait of a farmer carting pails of water. The bell above the door tinkled as she slipped out. Nick followed her to the glass door and looked around outside. Delson looked business as usual. He thought of what Jaqi would think of another body, and an arrest.

"Depends who they arrested," he said beneath his breath.

Three ad salespeople remained, though none were on the telephone, and none seemed to notice him. He thought to ask if they knew the name, but decided he wanted nothing to do with the sales force—mostly, they weren't like news people.

He wandered back the way he'd come, peeking into every dark office on his way by. Empty. He went to his soon-to-be former office and dialed Jaqi. She answered on the third ring.

"Hello?" she said.

"Did you hear?" he said.

"Oh my god! The mother was just on TV, then the chief. They brought in three guys, and for some reason they paraded them in front of cameras with handcuffs on. Pretty sure one was that pervy Ronald Adams."

Nick motor-boated his lips, thinking. "It's called a

perp walk and cops do it to poison the public well. If people see these guys in handcuffs, their first impression is guilt. Usually, they wait until they've been charged to walk them around like that. Did it say they were charged?"

"No. Should I call Allard?" Jaqi said, voice high, excited. "I bet those guys didn't do it."

"Sure, why not call, and who knows if they did."

He could almost hear her headshake despite the silence. "I was on my way out, too. I want to talk to some of the families."

"And say what?"

"We're working on a feature."

Nick rubbed his temple, weighing whether or not he thought Jaqi could handle it without proper training, then had to acknowledge that, compared to her, he was only slightly more equipped. A two-year college diploma program from a party school was hardly a Harvard Law degree.

"Just don't mention a specific paper."

"I was thinking of saying something like The Rolling Stone or Playboy," Jaqi said. "But if you don't think…"

Nick considered this and decided it was somewhere he'd better take a stand. "Don't lie. Twist and omit, okay, but let's not start outright lying to people who've lost a family member in this way. What do you think?"

Jaqi sighed. "You're right, but I'm on fire. This thing…we can find him. I feel it so deep. It's like I'm a volcano ready to burst. They arrested losers, not murderers. I know it!"

"Okay. Great. Just…be gentle and sort of honest about who the story is for. I mean, in reality, we might sell it to some huge place, but we have to get the story first."

"Yep, right. I'm going to call Allard. Love you."

Nick heard the pulse of a disconnected line in his ear. He had to laugh. He'd never been so gung-ho over a story. Never. He'd gotten into journalism because it sounded like more talking to people than working, going to sports events, checking out shitty high school plays; the existence of a truth people needed had never motivated him, had rarely come to mind.

"Could we really get him?" he said as he stepped into the breakroom to brew up a fresh pot of coffee.

As he sat, listening to the dribble and drip, he continued to wonder if Jaqi was right. Was it possible that they uncovered the identity when the cops couldn't? In another town it might seem silly, but with Rube, Rube the Tractor Tube at the helm, it not only sounded plausible, but likely.

He turned up the volume on the tape deck radio next to the microwave and listened. Something from Our Lady Peace was just concluding. Nick stiffened, as if any movement might scare away a news update. Blue Rodeo's slow and sappy *Try* began, and Nick relaxed. He'd just have to wait to know more.

26

Pierre Allard lived in a new townhouse along the eastern edge of Delson. Reprints of fine art hung along the main hallway walls that led from the foyer to the kitchen. The appliances were all name brand and the dining set looked like it carried a price tag comparable to the value of Jaqi's Honda Accord. The mugs they drank coffee from did not match the rest of the decor: Jaqi drank from a large, ceramic Garfield and Pierre drank from a large, plastic Wile E. Coyote mug with a nose that stretched about three inches from the face.

A small TV mounted beneath a cupboard faced the dining table where Jaqi and Pierre sat. They'd been discussing information that was technically public—if requested and approved after weeks of waiting—that Pierre could make copies of at work when the news conference appeared on the muted TV and he increased the volume.

"We have three men in custody, yes," Chief Thompson said. "And we're confident it will lead to an arrest."

"What about Stacy-Lynn Brown?" a feminine voice asked from beyond the camera range.

The chief ignored it.

"What are their names?" this from a man.

"Ronald Adams, twenty-nine, a known sexual offender; Michael, Mikey, Keane, twenty-five; and Jonathan, Jonny, Adams, twenty-five."

"What about Stacy-Lynn Brown?" asked that same feminine voice.

Once again, the chief ignored her.

"It doesn't make sense," Jaqi said.

Pierre looked at her, cocking his left eyebrow toward his hairline. "Oh?"

"Those guys might be skeevy pervs, but where would they keep the girls, and for ten, eleven months? How did they know where to sneak into and when? People would notice any of those sloppy guys hanging around their neighborhood. It can't be any of them. The Dollmaker is smart, patient, and has more means than those assholes will ever see." The moment she finished, a blush burned up her collar into her cheeks; she was an amateur talking to a pro; what the hell did she know?

Pierre grinned. "You're absolutely right. Of course, they need arrests or the public explodes, and likely Rube thinks he can pin another tail on another situationally innocent donkey."

"Like Donny Tiffany?"

Pierre snapped a finger gun at Jaqi.

"Did you know, shortly after Donny Tiffany was arrested, a girl went missing, but they didn't think it was connected, despite that a glasscutter was involved. They even ran it in the paper."

Now all the playfulness disappeared from Pierre's

face. "The glasscutter's being used now, too."

Jaqi nearly launched from her seat. "It's him! It's all one guy! It has to be a cop! Why is the truth being pushed away so much otherwise?"

Hand beneath his chin, elbow on the table, eyes gazing vacantly at the tall fence a dozen steps beyond his rear patio door, Pierre said, "I doubted it very much until this second...but they're all so thick. None of them could do it." He shook his head. "No, they're morons."

"Maybe not a current cop, but what about one from the 'eighties?"

"I got put on the evening shift due to uselessness. I'll find and print you a list tonight." Pierre huffed, grinning again. "Now you have me wishing I were on the case, too."

An advertisement for Crest toothpaste lit on the TV and Pierre hit the mute button on the little remote. He turned to face Jaqi dead on.

"You've been a fun surprise," he said.

Jaqi frowned. "Why did you become a cop? Did you lose your law license?"

Pierre pouted out his bottom lip and shook his head gently, somberly. "My grandfather was a cop, my dad was a cop, four of five uncles were or are cops; every one of them is an ignorant asshole. My father disowned me when my photo appeared on the front page of the Toronto Star for protesting police brutality at gay night clubs. They used to sting them, and every closeted man just trying to shave out a sliver of good in a bleak world was laid bare;

they'd lose families, jobs, and they'd—doesn't matter, I'm sure you know the shameful things cops have done. Anyway, on my father's deathbed I told him my plan to become a cop, just to observe and note. The Delson PD is about as dumb as it gets. They were the fifth station I tried after quitting law."

There was a frown on Jaqi's face. "Sounds like a lot to get even with a dead man."

Pierre burst out laughing. "That's exactly what my therapist said! You may not realize this, but humans are imperfect; and even intelligent, educated humans get to do dumb stuff if it makes them feel a little happy."

"Okay."

"Someday, you'll understand. More coffee?"

"Please," Jaqi said.

Pierre rose, taking both mugs with him to the percolator next to the microwave on the kitchen's island counter. "Now, what's got you so interested? Serial killers are a far reach from physical therapy."

"Yeah. I've never been so interested in anything. I've never been interested in murderers at all, really, then Nick and I devised—well, I guess I did… I came up with the idea that he tackle this story in real depth, sell it to a newspaper, then get a better job."

Pierre stirred cream into his coffee. "Doesn't like the Mirror?"

"It was fine, but he's fired at the end of the week."

"Ah, I guess that makes sense. Nobody in this town will forget that he printed that child's name. What an exceptionally unfortunate screw-up."

Jaqi accepted her steamy mug and put her lips between Garfield's ears as Pierre slipped back into his seat.

"That still doesn't explain your enthusiasm," Pierre said, then sipped.

"Guess it doesn't," Jaqi said, right index running rings around the rim of her goofy mug, "but I can't really explain it. It's like a compulsion. I just…just have to know and have to show. I mean, we could save a girl, maybe countless girls, all we have to do is put together the pieces. And, unlike the cops, we get to do it without consequences."

Pierre tipped his head left-right, right-left. "If you figure this out and make a police chief look bad, best mind the law, in Delson at least. I suppose you won't be here long though?"

She shook her head. "It was supposed to be me leaving at the end of August to finish school, but now I guess we could leave any time after Friday, and I think Nick will want to leave fairly quickly, but I'm not leaving until this thing is figured…well, not before the end of August."

Pierre leaned forward, taking up the blue ballpoint from next to a legal notepad. "Guess we'd better get this grocery list of info you need set for my next shift then, huh?"

27

For three straight days after the guys met in Kris Edler's garage for beers to hash out a plan, Pauline, Kris' fourteen-year-old daughter, sunbathed in the front yard wearing a two-piece bikini. And every night, Kris made like he was leaving for the bar, but instead parked a few blocks away and hitched a ride back to his block with one of the guys. One man remained stationed in the home, hidden away in the large living room closet where he had quick access to Pauline's stand-in, Pete, who would be wearing Pauline's clothes.

The police had claimed to have the guy, and that dulled some of the enthusiasm, but nobody truly believed it. Robert Thompson wasn't so much older that they didn't recall his goofy, nerdy self, back when *everyone* called him Rube, Rube the Tractor Tube to his face, before he became a cop, and certainly before he wormed his way into the chief of police position.

On the fourth night, a man finally appeared.

They kept the entire house dark but for the living room, and even there, they kept it dim. The TV was on at a slightly above normal volume and Andrei sat in the closet, penlight in one hand, a copy of *Hood* by Emma Donoghue in the other, all the time with an ear listening for change in the living room.

Outside, parked on the street in a van with deeply tinted windows were Zach and Kris. Colin had been the most rambunctious after hearing the plan, though couldn't be there tonight on account of covering another bus driver's route as a favor—trading shifts was regular thanks to a simple punch card system.

It was a little after 10:00 PM, Thursday night. The streetlights above the home flickered off a few moments before the old Ford pickup crept along, stopping in front of Kris' driveway. The driver killed the engine and got out with a pack slung over his shoulder. He stepped straight to the front door.

"Go time!" Zach said and burst out of the van; Kris close behind him. Both men had rifles in hand.

They watched as the man reached for the door. It was enough for Kris. He fired, pulled the bolt to eject the casing and chambered another round, fired again. The man didn't fully make it to the ground. He was slumped, his face pressed to the door.

"Holy fuck!" Zach shouted. "Holy fuck!"

The door opened and the man—almost a man—fell into the foyer, crushing his thermal pizza delivery bag in the process. There was a bill in his hand that, aside from the order itself, featured the address 696 Camber Street. Kris lived at 969 Camber Street.

Andrei rushed up, looked at the kid, then to Kris. Kris' triumph had disappeared and he now wore the ghoul mask of the horrifically guilty. Andrei grabbed Pete's slender wrist.

"We weren't here. There was no scheme to catch the killer. You saw a kid and got worried for your daughter. Zach, go fetch his daughter, fast, then go. I cannot go back," Andrei said, the words rushed, emotional, final.

Pete pulled his arm back a hair and his fingers slipped between Andrei's a moment before Andrei led the charge through the home to the back door. Andrei was parked around the block.

"You heard him," Kris said, then sank to his knees next to the dead boy and the ever-growing halo of blood surrounding him.

Zach rushed off. He didn't recall Kris' ex-wife's name, but knew the new husband, and he called for the girl. "That thing you've been helping your dad with, we have to do a little work tonight."

Pauline did not argue or waste time. The morning after the planning meeting, they'd paid Pauline $150 to do what she was told and ask no questions, and especially not tell anyone what she was doing. She had also weaseled a future house party out of her father in the deal, but that seemed highly unlikely now.

Police sirens were audible up the block by the time Zach and Pauline arrived. Zach had filled the girl in, but she didn't grasp the reality or severity of the situation until she saw her father crying over the dead body of Dan Lidster, a boy who was only just finishing a thirteenth year at her school to bump up his marks for college applications.

"Like I said: you were here all night, your dad just

stepped out a minute to pick up his rifle from me because I'd lost a bet and had to clean it. Got it?" Zach said, side-eying the flashing lights headed their way.

Pauline didn't answer, enrapt by the scene at her feet.

"Got it?" Zach said, taking her shoulder and shaking her.

"Yes," she whispered, voice barely audible.

"Okay. You got that, Kris? I lost a bet and had to clean your rifle, that's why you stepped out, and when you saw the kid—"

Kris whirled around, face wet with tears and blood—he'd obviously touched the kid—and shouted, "Got it! Now, fuck off!"

Zach did as told, pulling away in the borrowed van just as three cop cars and an ambulance appeared on the street. Neighbors streamed from their homes, as if the law arriving was their personal invitation. Inside five minutes, Zach was sitting in his usual seat at The Bruce, sipping a beer, staring up at the highlights from the Blue Jays game.

—

Andrei took Pete back to his home. Pete was quiet, in shock. Andrei got him out of Pauline's clothes, and into his bed. Moments later, Andrei spooned his naked body behind Pete's and draped an arm over him.

"It's going to be okay," Andrei said, then gently kissed Pete's ear.

They'd been quietly meeting since the second night Pete had been in town.

"I don't want to go back to prison. I can't. I make

jokes, but it's the scariest place in the world."

"Hush," Andrei said, kissing Pete on the lips this time to silence him.

"Just hold me, tonight," Pete said.

"Of course," Andrei said.

28

"Hey, Nick? You mind forgetting about the scanning today and grab some streeters? With Martine out of the picture and all that's going on, we could use a little help," Eugene said.

Nick had made it only as far as the breakroom and was pouring a cup of coffee when the editor came in sporting well-worn saddlebags beneath his eyes and a pallor like mozzarella cheese. As for the request, Nick hadn't planned on doing much scanning; for the last two days he mostly sat down in the dark, dank basement thinking about the information they'd amassed, trying to put the pieces together. He also spent a great deal of time wondering what Jaqi was up to; once, his thoughts of Jaqi got away from him and he imagined him, Jaqi, and a young woman who worked overnights at 7-Eleven in a threesome and he'd had to scurry up to the bathroom to masturbate into a urinal.

"Okay," Nick said, stepping away.

"And Nick?" Eugene said—Nick paused his exit. "I'm sorry this didn't work out."

"Right," Nick said, adjusting his messenger bag. He carried on, hooking a left instead of a right out of the breakroom.

After a few steps, the door at the end of the hall opened and a strangely familiar looking young woman with huge glasses stepped into the Mirror office.

"Do I just go back?"

"Yep. Eugene's back there somewhere," Erica said from the sales bullpen.

As they drew closer, then passed one another, something clicked for both and they looked over their shoulders almost simultaneously. Nick did not know her name, but he'd met her three times at different program parties, and once more in the newsroom—by the end of first year, most students had stories in the school paper, though the second-year students operated the ins and outs. She was a year lower than him at Fanshawe, meaning she was only just graduated.

Nick hurried his steps; the last thing he needed was to be saddled with a trainee, explaining the great intricacies of asking the general public random, mostly meaningless, questions.

A few meters from the Mirror's entry was a Bell Telephone booth. Seeing it flashed an idea upon Nick and he called home. When it came to Streeters, it hardly mattered who he questioned, as long as he could get a picture and enough quotes to fill a box. Typically, they ran five or six a week, which allowed them to produce more pages that could be filled with advertising; readers might get aggravated with five or six pages of nothing but classifieds and general advertising, but they wouldn't if each of those pages had some news-adjacent content and pictures of people they'd likely seen around town.

He stepped into the steamy little booth and cringed as he punched the number to reach Jaqi at the apartment. A demand for payment flashed as he fished in his pocket for a quarter. The coin clinked down into the hungry belly of the telephone. Nick held the receiver a few centimeters from his face.

"Hello?" Jaqi said.

"Hey, it's me. Can you give me the names and places where I might reach those former cops? I got sent out to do streeters, might as well do two tasks at once."

"Does this mean you're not getting fired?"

Nick, no longer thinking about germs or the nastiness of public telephones, pinched the receiver between his shoulder and ear as he dug into his bag for a pen and notepad. "No, I'm still fired. They brought in this chick who was a year behind me at Funshawe."

"Oh, ah, okay. Pierre called me; guess some idiots tried to catch the Dollmaker and killed a pizzaman. He's coming by to check our progress. Okay, here, you ready?" Jaqi rattled off the names and Nick got to work looking for the four men.

—

Cory Corriveau was the first name on the list. He'd been fired from the police department for marijuana use—specifically, the use of marijuana from the evidence locker. He'd gone on to start a small press in his basement, and that was where the information stopped.

"So, you're from the Mirror, huh?" he said. He was a biggish sort, fatty rather than muscly.

"That's right. Can you tell me what you think of the current social climate in Delson?" Nick said, holding out his tape recorder, which was now the elder of two available to him as Jaqi had one as well.

"People seem scared and angry."

"Scared generally? And angry at whom?"

Cory nodded as he took a deep drag from a cigarette. "Scared generally. I'm guessing old Rube saw his waning days coming and arrested those idiots to save his ass; anybody with half a brain can see that. I used to be a police officer."

Nick put on an intrigued expression. "Really?"

"Yep. Got canned because I stole back a bag of pot another cop confiscated from my buddy. I didn't take it until the crown attorney decided he wasn't going to charge anyone." Cory shrugged. "But pot's illegal for some dumb reason."

"So, you don't think Robert Thompson is up to this challenge?"

Cory started to laugh somewhere in his sinus, a little grunting sound. "I don't want the aggravation that would follow answering that question from a reporter."

PAINTED DEAD GIRLS

"Okay, what if I was putting together a different story, for a different paper, what do you think of the chief?"

"This won't be printed in the Mirror?"

"Not unless the story comes out elsewhere and someone at the Mirror quotes from it, but that seems like a longshot. They're not much into deep diving over there."

Cory thought a moment, eyes glassy and unfocussed. "All right. Let me just tell you a story about Rube, Rube the Tractor Tube."

"I'm ready," Nick said when Cory paused for more than a ten count.

Blinking rapidly, Cory snapped himself from reverie. "In twelfth grade, there were two or three losers, like, I mean super losers. Rube was easily in the bottom two: fat, pimply, balding, smelly, cheap clothes, bad grades, ate stuff like headcheese and pickle sandwiches, a total social misfit. Anyway, I was in ninth grade at the time, and they were remodeling one wing of the school, so sometimes rooms had to pull double duty. So, my ninth-grade gym class had to share the changeroom with a twelfth-grade gym class. Near the end of class, this dopey kid—he'd dropped out before getting to tenth grade—kicked a basketball across the gym from the doorway of the equipment room and nailed me in the face—we were playing floor hockey; like, the class was, I mean. My glasses broke and I had a bloody nose, so I went back to the changeroom. I heard him before I saw him. There was this whining voice saying, 'fucking idiot, fucking loser, fucking fat loser,' stuff like that. Then I heard these smacks. I don't know if it's good or bad that the door made no noise, but anyway, there's Rube, smacking the side of his head, muttering to himself, standing in only his tighty-whities, big, heavy skid mark riding the off-white canvas like spilled pudding. His corduroy shorts were around his ankles, shit smeared, too."

"Yee," Nick said from the core of a grimace.

"Yeah, man. So, Rube goes around to the various piles of clothes and finds some that fit him, leaving his shit-stained undies behind, in the pile where he stole a pair of jeans. I bolted out of there, fighting off a laugh. It was so fucked up. My brother stopped me on the way—now this bit, I'm ashamed of having any part of, but the prick deserved it. My brother was doing a grade thirteen year; right then he was smoking darts with some of the other seniors in the student lounge. He shouted at me and I raced in to tell him, then he made me show him. After that I ran up to the gym to tell my teacher that Rube Thompson stole this other kid's pants; this other kid was named Rudy; he was all right."

Nick was already guessing where this was going.

"So, anyway, gym teacher leaves us a minute and I'm retelling the scene to my classmates. Oh! And it was last period. Teacher comes back, tells us all to go change, and while we're heading down, the vice principal gets on the PA system asking that Robert Thompson go to the office. Few minutes later, the hallways are full of laughter, kids rushing along to the doors. I followed the flow out front, wondering what the hell was going on. Then I see Rube's shitty drawers way up the flagpole. And then there's Rube, in his dirty corduroy shorts, vice principal behind him. Dude made Rube bring his undies down off the flagpole. Took him like five minutes to figure out the rope."

The only response coming to Nick was to shake his head, so he did.

"Now, get me, what I did wasn't cool. What my brother and his friends did wasn't cool. But, how fucked up is a guy that would shit his self, steal someone else's pants, then leave his nasty drawers on someone else's stuff? Like, was he hoping this other fat kid had to get it like him? Or did he not even consider the drawers after he dropped them? I should've known it was a trick when he made a point of telling me specifically that he forgot to lock the evidence locker one day when I was ending my shift, and he was just heading out. That cunt."

"Wow," Nick said, then, pulling it back to more pertinent facts, "What did you do after you were fired?"

"Went to the Klondike with a mining upstart. I invested three grand, what was left of my pension after I cashed out early. Made a ton of money. I came back in 'eighty-five and started Gold Mine Publishing. That gold money is the only way I can do it. Gets harder and harder every year. Last year I made like fourteen grand, not quite enough to cover all my living expenses, but pretty close."

Nick was only vaguely listening, mentally crossing Cory Corriveau off his list. "What kinds of books did you say?" he said as he clicked stop on his recorder.

ATLAS WUNDOR

Six minutes later, Nick departed the man's home with a little more insight into Delson's chief of police, a potential suspect stroked off his list, and a copy of a hardcover book titled *Rabid Mammoths of the Great White North* by C. Ernest Corriveau.

—

It was 11:19 AM when he reached the home of Elton Meyers. The man was in a wheelchair—an arrant 2x4 had ended his police career when it fell from some high scaffolding and hit him, moving straight down, in the top of his spine. He could walk with two canes on good days, but he hadn't been able to feel his feet since 1984. Nick, beyond his control, tried to imagine the man and his 90-pound wife doing the deed and swatted it away. Still, there were questions to ask.

"Wait, are you trying to suggest that retard was innocent?" Elton's expression balled tight toward the center of his face. "He confessed."

The temperature was on the cusp of getting instantly hot, so Nick backed it up; angry interviewees were typically all but useless in a situation like this.

"No, I'm writing a story about a small city plagued by murders. Rube—Robert Thompson was in charge or was among the arresting officers on several cases now."

The anger fleeted and Elton sank into his chair. "In a perfect world, a better cop would have his job. In a perfect world, good cops could stay on the job for life."

Nick nodded, hit stop on his recorder, and rose. "That's all I need. Thank you for your time."

Elton's wife appeared beneath the arched entrance to the living room holding a trey of tea and digestive biscuits. "You're leaving?" she said.

She looked so sad and desperate that Nick tapped a finger against his chin, then said, "Well actually—just thought of this—I'm supposed to grab some streeters. We can pretend this is a street, yeah?"

She smiled widely and Elton grinned, looking at his wife's face.

—

1:24 PM, Nick found Luke Craven at work at the Home Hardware, stacking boxed hockey helmets into an off-season sale display. He'd called Luke's home, spoke with the man's girlfriend while eating a sandwich and a Ziploc baggy of Lay's Ketchup chips. That section of the store smelled of leather and rubber, enough so that it drowned out the general sawdust scent of the building.

"Luke?" Nick said.

The man straightened and turned in a single smooth motion. He was tall, his arms roped by veins, a gut drooping over his beltline. There was a rigid burn scar slicing from his right ear, under his nose, down to the left side of his jaw.

Nick had seen enough malady and misfortune to keep from reacting to that kind of surprise.

"Yeah, can I help you?"

Nick quickly filled in the sum of what he'd told the others. Twice customers stopped at the helmet display to snatch one up—30% off. When he was done, he waited for a response from Luke.

"I don't even like to think about those days." Luke absently touched his scar. "I got into the cops and decided it was all sitting around doing nothing, so I quit and joined the fire department. I wanted to be a hero. First housefire? I trip, helmet wasn't strapped because I thought it looked cooler open, fall face first into the flames." He shook his head.

"That's terrible."

Luke pulled his lips back into a deep frown. "Well, yes and no. Met my wife. She was a new nurse and had to tend to me for three weeks." He sighed. "Wish I could've met her some other way. You did a good job, but your eyes flashed just a hair. Kids stare like crazy. Now and then, adults actually cringe ."

No chance you're walking around a neighborhood without being remembered, Nick thought, then said, "Oh, I'm sorry. I wasn't expecting—"

"A glaring abnormality?" Luke said, putting extra emphasis on each syllable of abnormality.

Nick stiffened. "I suppose."

Luke sighed once more. "I don't remember much about being a cop, was only there a year and a half or so, and I was mostly worried about screwing blue bunnies."

"Blue bunnies?"

Luke huffed and got back to stacking helmets. "Girls who fuck cops because they're cops. Blue bunnies, like puck bunnies. Just what we called them."

Nick thanked him for his time and exited the

hardware store. There was just one name remaining on his list, and he'd have to wait for a call back or try again himself. Apparently, this Kris Edler ran his own electrician business.

Before he headed back to the office, he rolled over to the high school. Around back, where the greasers loitered, cigarettes burning endlessly, he found three willing interviewees. He snapped photos to go along with the quotes, then returned to the office.

29

What Jaqi was doing did not match up to what she'd told Nick. Whether he realized it or not, this now had nothing to do with a story for her. She went to the home of Melissa Sparks first. Renee was a wreck, but more than willing to talk. Jaqi only had to say the story would likely print in a larger paper than the Mirror and *open sesame*…the woman talked and talked and talked.

First thing that morning Jaqi had called Pierre. They'd met for coffee, and he gave her tips on getting facts out of people and gave a few tidbits on the tendencies of repetitive criminals, especially those involving murder or arson.

"Can you think back to around the days or weeks

preceding your daughter's disappearance—"

"She was taken; she didn't disappear."

"Of course, forgive me."

Renee, face puffy, eyes looking sleep deprived, sipped from her mug, staring vacantly into the distance. Jaqi tried to imagine how this woman felt and realized, if she was lucky, she'd never be able to relate.

"In the days and weeks preceding…did you see any police officers hanging around the neighborhood?"

This snapped Renee from reverie. "I did. I don't know his name."

Jaqi swallowed down a monstrous wave of excitement. "Could you pick out his picture, from a group of them, I mean?"

"Probably."

Jaqi rooted through the folders she'd stuffed into her big purse—three times the size of her usual purse. It was leather with frills cut along the edges, which made her think of skinny fingers. She placed pictures of the current police force—provided by Pierre Allard—before the woman. Renee leaned forward, looking for more than a minute before bringing up her face, expression bearing a confused frown.

"He's not here."

"You're sure?"

"Yeah, he had a moustache, but not big and gawdy like these three. It was full and straight, a regular moustache. You know?"

Nodding, Jaqi said, "Interesting. Okay. Did you see

anybody else in the neighborhood?"

"Well, yeah. The ice cream truck came by, and they arrested him, but where's my girl?" Renee began breathing heavier and heavier until she was on the brink of hyperventilating.

Jaqi popped from her spot on the couch to sit next to Renee on the love seat. She rubbed her back, whispering, "Breathe, breathe, breathe."

Once Renee recovered herself, she rose abruptly and started for her bedroom. The door closed. Jaqi waited a few minutes, weighing whether or not to ask Renee if she was going to be okay. In the end, she gathered all she'd laid out for the woman to consider and left.

—

Stacy-Lynn Brown's parents were home together, both on an extended leave from jobs at the casket factory. They were doing better than Renee Sparks, possibly because they had closure, possibly because they had each other, possibly because they were still in shock.

"There are cops around sometimes lately, I guess. They got the guys, though, didn't they?" Frank said. "That ice cream truck was here all the damned time, motherfucking pervert sonofabitch."

"There's been arrests, sure. I'm just building a story. Do you think you'd recognize the police who were around if I showed you pictures?"

Jamie rubbed her forehead gently. "Maybe."

"You think it was a cop?" Frank said as Jaqi laid out the photocopies of headshots from the station's records.

"I'm gathering information. Some neighborhoods have a police presence, and some don't," Jaqi said, offering up a response she'd had canned and ready.

"Oh, okay," Frank said.

Jamie and Frank scanned the pictures slowly, going over them once, twice, thrice before looking at one another. Jamie was the first to look to Jaqi, as if she might have an answer.

"The one with the moustache isn't here."

Adrenaline filled Jaqi. It felt as if someone had plugged her in, let electricity slip through her in white hot pulses. She took a single deep breath before she asked if they were certain.

"Half these guys were here after—" Jamie stopped herself, hand going to her stretching mouth as a deep, pained howl rode up her throat.

Frank pulled her to his shoulder. "I guess it could be any of the ones without moustaches, if they grew one and shaved it."

Some of the excitement slipped away within Jaqi. That was logical, likely even. "Aside from the officer you saw, and the ice cream truck, who else comes around here who doesn't live in the park?"

"Like who?"

"I don't know, garbagemen?"

Frank wrinkled his brow. "Nah, the garbage is picked up like every three weeks. We have a big dumpster out front of the park. Garbage truck doesn't even come through the gates." He tipped his head and pouted his lips.

"Same for the city bus. There's a stop across the street, but buses don't go into parks. Sometimes there's an electrician or something, usually Kris Edler. He's a bit of a drunk, but pretty reliable. He's good buddies with that Zach Soderberg, you know, who shot the pizza guy? That's tough, the way everybody's feeling and everything going on, I don't really blame him for being trigger happy."

"Was the electrician around here recently?" Jaqi said.

Jaqi hadn't thought of private service people; government workers and imposters of such, she and Nick had considered that, but it was so big and none of the people either had spoken with had mentioned a meter reader or a city works employee, not even a cable guy had been around in the dozens of other scenarios they'd questioned people about. Expanding the possibilities would open the door on countless potential suspects, and she didn't dare let it side track her from the moustachioed cop angle.

"Uh, maybe?" Frank said. "Look, you've upset us. Do you mind doing this some other time?"

"Oh, no, of course. I'm sorry…I'm sorry for your loss," Jaqi said.

Jamie snapped her face around. "You're sorry, huh? Here trying to make money off our story and you're sorry?" The venom was thick, spittle misting from her dry and peeling lips.

"Babe," Frank said, pulling Jamie tighter to his side.

Jamie shook herself free. "You're sorry? Get the fuck

out of here!"

Jaqi leapt to her feet. She scrambled to gather the photographs she'd spread on the scuffed coffee table. "I didn't mean to upset you," she said under her breath.

"Just go," Frank said as Jamie melted into sobs against his shoulder.

Everything loaded into her purse, Jaqi hurried away without another word.

30

The Dollmaker in his ski mask uncuffed Melissa Sparks' ankles from the cot. It was the same every day, and she didn't even fight it anymore. She didn't kick out or fidget, she simply let him cuff her; when he was done with her makeup—he'd only done her nails once, so far—standing naked and damp before her, she'd lie still until he was through raping her. That ski mask gave her hope that this was only temporary, even when that mummified corpse set into the wall suggested that this was forever.

But why would he cover his identity if he was just going to murder her?

She'd been in captivity at least a week, though it felt like several weeks, a month even. Every day was long. She lay in bed reading musty paperbacks, constantly distracted by the daily visits where the Dollmaker would cuff her, fix her makeup, assault her, then leave her be until supper. His method was brief, at least. It wasn't about torture, it was about something else, something that refused to piece together.

"He wants you pregnant," she said then, after hours of deep thought.

Melissa had been talking to herself more and more each day. And she hadn't heard another voice since those screams ceased days ago.

"These walls are tough," she said as she slipped into cotton pajama pants provided by the Dollmaker, her back pressed into the unforgiving paneling. "But what about that cell in the wall?"

Melissa had looked at the freakish display twice but hadn't dared touch the bars. Now, she dropped to her knees and slid beneath the cot. It was so clean down there. No dust bunnies, no insects, not even a crack in the cement.

Settled on her tummy, Melissa looked at the corpse and the bars. The mummy had a leathery scent with hints of spices and dirt, noticeable only because she was so close. Slowly, meekly, Melissa reached for the bars. The steel was unexpectedly cool beneath her touch. She jerked her hand to her mouth, as if burnt.

She closed her eyes, imagining the steel falling away, imagining dragging the old corpse out, imagining pushing away the second set of bars. She'd be out. The other side would be part of the greater building, a part with an exit.

She'd get outside and run and run and run. The sun would blind her momentarily with its beauty. She'd make it home and kiss her mother. She'd make it home and call the police. She'd make it home and be her the way she was before her life was stolen and soured by a masked predator.

"Okay," she whispered. "They'll move."

She reached again, grasped a bar, and tugged.

Not even a hint of movement. She pulled her hands away, momentarily defeated, then, screaming, frantic, desperate, Melissa grasped the bars, shaking her entire body, using her legs for leverage, shifting angles. Nothing worked. Suddenly, she quieted and slid out from beneath the cot.

Pillow propped behind her where she lay, she cracked open yet another Agatha Christie novel and read.

31

After work, Nick had to meet the final former police officer on the list, an electrician named Kris Edler. Nick had called home and left a message on the machine before he departed the busy office. The staff was alive with action—even the new girl was getting bylines—murders, accidental death, arrests, the Mirror had had a week, including the ad staff. Nothing brought advertisers like eyeballs; nothing brought eyeballs like salacious stories that spurred fear amid the general population.

"Good luck out there," Eugene said from the breakroom as Nick snuck toward the rear door.

Nick stopped, took three backward steps, and popped his head into the breakroom. "Thanks. See you around, man."

Eugene saluted him, unlit cigarette dangling from his bottom lip. He was in the midst of fixing a mug of coffee.

So, that was it. Nick was unemployed. He stepped out into the hot early evening and lit a cigarette. He puffed as he took the long route around the block, hoping to avoid anyone else from the Mirror. There was a flyer for half-price tandoori buffet beneath the driver's side wiper of his car. "Huh," he said, unaware that Delson had an Indian joint.

He had twenty minutes before he had to meet the electrician, so he pulled into the liquor store parking lot. He'd need supplies if he was going to have a minor, somber unemployment party for himself. Crossing the lot, he tossed his cigarette butt ahead of him, toed it out, and carried onward.

The LCBO liquor store was cool beyond the automatic doors. Two teenagers stood by a beer cooler, each holding a forty of Olde English, discussing whether or not they dared try a can of the German motor oil called Faxe. Nick wanted to encourage them—he'd downed a handful of cans of the 10% atrocity a few times, back in his college days—but passed them by. He wouldn't be there to see their faces after that first sip anyway.

He reached the tequila bottles, snatched up a bottle of Cazadores, a surprisingly inexpensive and yet smooth offering in a sea of more famous, and decidedly gross, tequilas. Not sure how much vodka they had left, he grabbed a bottle of Polar Ice as well. Getting wasted alone was not the party he had in mind.

The boys with the beers were at the till and the woman on cash was giving them a hard time. Only one had ID and, according to this woman, it wasn't wholly convincing.

"Street?"

"Thirteen-twelve Oxford," the one teen said.

"Date of birth?"

"May seventh, seventy-eight."

The woman snatched up a notepad and pen. "Let's see your signature."

"Fine," the teen said, accepting the pen and writing his name with little pause.

The woman eyed it like it was a thousand-dollar bill needing verified. From an office, a younger woman popped her head and left shoulder out. "Just sell them the beer. He's been coming in almost every day since his birthday."

The teens grinned. The woman working the till scowled.

Nick leaned in behind the teens as the woman bagged the beer. "That Faxe shit is gnarly."

The one without a card turned with a smile. "You've

partaken?"

Nick laughed. "Unfortunately. Drink lots of water before you go to bed."

"Ten-four, Kemosabe."

"Next," the woman working the till said. "ID?"

The teens moved on and Nick presented his license. The woman gave it a cursory glance, then handed it back. "You still at the paper?" she said, explaining why he didn't get at least a bit of a rougher ride—he wasn't that far removed from his teens.

"No, today was my last day."

"Good. Thirty-nine-fifty," she said, bagging the bottles.

Nick dug free two twenties from his wallet. "You must be a hoot at parties," he said.

"I wouldn't want to be at any parties you'd be at," she said as she made change.

Nick took the matching paper bags, then the quarters. "That's perfect because you'd never be welcome at any parties I'd attend."

"You should've been charged for what you did to that innocent girl. She'd been through enough and you, what? Thought you get a stir up for the paper?"

"It was an accident. Same thing your mother said when she found out she was pregnant with you."

Nick hurried off, champion of jabs, before a good rebuttal could come his way. The liquor went into the trunk. According to his Timex, he had more than ten minutes to get about three minutes away. He hurried over to the Becker's Milk Co. next-door to the liquor store, grabbed a bottle of cranberry juice and two packs of smokes. There was no fuss and even less conversation from the frumpy man operating the till.

When Nick arrived at his destination, Kris Edler was unloading trash from the back of his pickup truck. Nick pulled to the shoulder on the street by the man's driveway to park. Pen, pad, recorder in hands, Nick exited his car. A big, winning smile filled the bottom of his face.

"Hi. Nick Price."

The electrician did a half-turn, arms loaded with plastic and cardboard. He stuffed the trash into a white, five-gallon pale at his feet. "You're the newspaper guy?"

"That's right," Nick said, immediately feeling guilty for lying.

"Okay. So, what was this about the 'eighties?"

On the message he'd left, Nick explained that he was getting stories from people who were around during the first string of murders, especially those who'd formally been involved in law enforcement.

"Come ask while I'm cleaning up."

Kris led the way into his large garage. There was a wall of plastic treys, a massive Snap-on toolbox, and several large spools of wire, in various colors and thicknesses. On a work bench were tools, zip ties, an assortment of tapes, and a handful of strange—strange to Nick—digital meters and readers in bright orange and yellow shells. There was also a van with blackout tinted windows. Hanging on nails were a series of baseball caps and a single, black ski mask.

"Close that door," Kris said. "You're letting in the heat."

The garage was cooler, but not *that* much cooler. Still, Nick stepped inside and closed the door behind him.

32

Jaqi called the police station, leaving a message for Pierre to reach her at home. Twenty minutes later, as she stood before the wall of evidence, the buzzer sounded. She rushed into the kitchen, pressed the button, and said, "Yes?"

"This is Pierre Allard."

"Oh, do you want to come up?"

"Better than talking to this box."

"Right, of course." Jaqi pressed the button to release the lock downstairs.

She waited by the door, listening for the elevator bell. It chimed and she opened the apartment door. Pierre was headed her way, studying the walls, the rug, the ceiling.

"Hey," Jaqi said, suddenly self-conscious that the building wasn't all that nice compared to his digs—this despite that he'd already seen the place.

"I didn't know you well enough to ask before, but

have you ever been on the eighth floor?" Pierre said as he drew closer.

Leading the mini parade into the apartment, Jaqi said, "Nope."

"It's completely renovated. Only four apartments up there. All four bedroom, two bath, big den, massive places for this kind of building." Pierre closed the door behind him. "I looked at one when I moved to town. All hardwood and stainless-steel."

Jaqi led the way into the living room. "That'd be nice."

The conversation instantly shifted without another word on the building. Pierre stepped up to the evidence wall and looked at what Jaqi and Nick had gathered.

"This is good," Pierre said. "Why'd you call?"

Jaqi took a deep breath. "Renee Sparks recalled seeing an officer around in the days preceding her daughter's disappearance. Kidnapping. Jamie and Frank, Stacy-Lynn's parents, saw an officer. All three said the officer had a moustache, and all three said the officer did not match any of the photos I showed them. I showed them all the pictures you gave me."

Pierre rubbed his chin, making a subtle bristling sound with his five o'clock shadow. "Now, that's interesting."

"Frank Wilson, Stacy-Lynn's step…dad, her mom's boyfriend, said he also saw an electrician named…" Jaqi flipped through a small notepad. "Named Kris Edler. Kris Edler, that sounds familiar."

Pierre shrugged. "I know him to see him. I've seen his

van and his truck around, usually parked outside The Bruce." Pierre closed his left eye, frowning. "Now that I think about it, he pals around with Zack Soderberg."

"Right, the guy who shot the pizzaman. But there's something else. I've seen his name." Jaqi gazed vacantly at the floor, trying to connect misplaced dots. "Maybe it was just around, I guess."

Pierre leaned closer to the map. "What's Nick up to? Still at work?"

"He should be home by now. It was his last day," Jaqi said. "Do you want something to drink?"

"No, thank you." Pierre stepped to the patio door and looked out into the bright evening.

The shadow he cast made Jaqi think of late-night boogeymen creeping from shadows after cutting through glass to access locks and a chill danced her spine. The clock on the VCR/DVD player read: 06:19 PM.

Nick should've been home a while ago now. It felt like they were getting close, close to a killer. Her palms began to sweat.

33

Kris Edler pulled a box cutter from his pocket. "You think those murders are connected to these murders?" He thumbed the blade in and out as he spoke.

"Not necessarily. Murders have an affect on the world

around them. Double that in a place as small as Delson," Nick said, eyes glued to the pale blade.

"Ah," Kris said, then tossed the box cutter onto his messy workbench. "And you want a bit of insider information on police procedure, or what? I can't talk about a lot of things."

"Did you work any of the cases?"

Kris puffed out his chest. "Of course...I was on most of the search parties."

"Why did you leave?"

That puffed chest deflated some. "Wasn't for me...didn't make it past the six months probation. See, I used to have a drinking problem. I only drink beer, now, but back then... It ruined my chance to be a cop. Ruined my marriage, too."

Something tickled and tumbled in Nick's guts. "Too bad you have to turn in the uniform and badge, huh? Could have some fun goofing on people."

A strange grin came upon Kris' face. "Don't print this, but a buddy got a hold of a full set of cherries. We wired them onto a white Ford LTD. We'd go out and sit on the edge of the road and pull people over, looking for carloads of chicks. Sometimes one of us would wear the uniform and give the drivers a bitch of a time. Don't repeat that."

Nick plastered a near-perfect facsimile of an impressed, entertained smirk. "What did you do with the uniform and shield, then?"

Kris turned away, began sorting through the pail of

trash from his workday. "No idea; maybe I gave them back and forgot; maybe we burned them one night, used to have some raging bonfires at my buddy's parents' farm. I haven't seen the uniform or the shield in like…shit, I guess thirteen, fourteen years."

Something about the way he said this rang false with Nick. He'd spoken with countless people, and now and then, they'd realize they've overshared and clam up. Practiced or not, it was virtually impossible to crack them back open on short notice.

"You didn't just vacuum seal it away or something."

Kris slammed a handful of trash into a can next to his workbench. "What the hell did I just say?"

"Right, sorry. So, what happened after the police department?"

"Thought this was about dead girls?"

Nick shrugged, pretending to be interested in the bikini-clad Snap-on pinups on the walls. "It is. I'm just curious. It seems like a step up, becoming an electrician."

Kris took the bait. "Sure. It really did work out in the end, but right after they canned me, only thing I could get was pumping gas. That worked out, too, eventually. Guy's dad I knew from grade school stopped by and told me about an apprenticeship opportunity. I got it and here we are."

Nick nodded. "Right on. So, do you remember much about the days surrounding those disappearances and then finding the bodies, what was the social atmosphere, I mean?"

"Shit. Women were totally terrified. Dads too, I guess." Kris stepped to an old green fridge and swung open the door. He grabbed a bottle of Busch. "Want one?"

Before he could answer, a feminine voice drifted in from the driveway: "Nick? Nick?"

He pouted his bottom lip.

"You're Nick, yeah?"

Nick headed for the door. "I am."

He looked through a window. Jaqi was over by the house, looking in windows and calling, "Nick?"

"That your girlfriend?"

"Yeah. Say, thanks for your time. I'd better go see what she wants."

Kris twisted the cap from his bottle, took a swig, then said, "That's all you wanted to know?"

Nick opened the door. "Unless you know who the killer is?"

That brought about an amused tut. "If I knew, I'd sell that shit to the highest bidder."

"Me too," Nick said. "Thanks again."

Door closed behind him, Nick hurried to Jaqi who was squatting at the side of the house, next to a basement window. She jumped when he grabbed her forearm.

"You're okay," she said through a sigh.

"Of course I am. Come on, follow me home."

"It's him. Does he have a big, plain moustache?"

Nick stopped. They were about ten steps from the garage door. "Yes?" he whispered.

"A man dressed as a cop was seen around both the

Sparks and Brown homes. He had a moustache. I showed them pictures of every member of the Delson PD, well the cops. He wasn't there." She paused then, her expression skewing from certainty. "One saw an electrician…but, if he saw this guy, he'd recognize him in a uniform, right?"

Nick gave Jaqi a gentle shove toward the street. "Talk at home."

34

"You talk to Zach?" Kris said. He was on his usual stool, eyes on the TV above the wall of liquor bottles. The Expos were in San Fransisco, up 19-3 in the eighth inning.

Zach was still in lock-up while the Crown Attorney decided whether or not to charge him with anything—public opinion was in the air, though that was only because they didn't know the truth. Andrei hadn't been around in a few days—Pete had loose lips and now it was common knowledge that Andrei was gay—saying it was to his benefit that they were homophobes, however, that life wasn't meant to be wasted at a dive bar anyway.

"Not in a couple days," Colin said, then took a long swig from his bottle.

"Guess that kid's mother was let in to talk to him. She slapped him."

Colin nodded. Made sense. "Yeah."

"He tried to press charges against her."

Colin jerked his head right. "Fuck off."

"Seriously. I hate to think it, but the guy isn't who he was back in the day. Remember when he convinced that carload of chicks from OS to go out to your parents' farm by promising a spectacle—"

Colin slapped his thigh. "And he lit that stack of snowmobile crates on fire and danced at the top! Geez, that was something."

"Then he rolled that fucking tractor tire in."

"That one chick!" Colin said, almost vibrating on his stool.

"The rubber smoke. Oh god, what a hilarious canvas for all that rubber smoke."

"Looked like a goddamned zebra; the streaks she had…perfection."

Zach sighed. "I get that a divorce can be tough, but shit. I been divorced, you been divorced, didn't do a thing funny to us."

"Well, might've bothered me more if Jessica hadn't moved to the US."

"Nah," Zach said, "better if you see them get older and fatter. Every time I see Tasha and that clown she married, and those ugly goddamned kids, I thank the universe for my luck."

"I saw Tasha the other day. She's big, but that face is still pretty."

The men then sat in silence for the time it took Lee

Smith to record a strikeout and force a pop fly. The inning ended, the camera panning over a virtually empty stadium, only the diehards remaining in attendance…and a smattering of Expos fans. An ad for Burger King lit on the screen, a deconstructed burger being reconstructed while a woman sang about getting what she wanted.

"I remember the first time I saw Tasha. It was at that dance at Sacred Heart, you went, didn't you?" Zach said.

"Nah. My mom was funny about dances and stuff."

Zach frowned deeply, unintentionally bobbing his head to OMC's *How Bizarre*, which was pumping from the bar's stereo. "We were like eighteen by then?"

"Yeah, but Mom was sick, remember?"

"Ah, right."

Kris took a sip from his bottle. "I didn't see her again until like a month later at a kegger you had. It was the one where Tony Featherstone crashed his dad's Audi and punctured a lung."

Colin hissed through tight lips. "The prick dad tried to sue us because his son drank beer and drove."

"Fucking stupid. That barn was perfect for sleeping. You ever sell the property?"

"I wanted to, but I get sentimental. Totally overgrown now. The house had to come down, remember?"

"Sure, you let me take that wash sink from the laundry room. What about the fallout shelter. That was crazy. I had a secret plan, if the Russians dropped some bombs I was going straight out there."

Colin snorted, grinning with only the left side of his

mouth. "Think that was most people's plans. I haven't been down there in forever. I cleaned out the food, by and by. I ate a can of Spam from the 'seventies, well, took a bite...tossed everything after that."

"Ha. That's one thing I miss: home cooking. Tasha could cook."

"Same with Jessica."

Rod Beck took the mound, looking less than enthusiastic to have to be a part of the atrocious effort from a top-tier team. On the stereo was something slightly heavy and a bit grungy from Junkhouse. At the back, two dudes were clanging pool balls around a table drunkenly, sounding as if nobody was winning or ever would. Lexy was at the quiet corner of the bar, reading a Tim Wynne-Jones novel titled *The Maestro* beneath the lamp that typically shined on the till.

A failing bar going through its motions.

"Well," Zach said.

"Well," Colin said.

35

Melissa Sparks awoke to the sound of the door slowly clapping open, unsure of the time or how long she'd slept or how long she'd been away from home. She hadn't cried since after the first time the Dollmaker raped her, but now, she was unable to quit crying.

"Mommy, Mommy, Mommy," she moaned as she rocked on the cot.

The feeding slot in the door was down, and on it was a tin plate with a fork and a serving of nasty, chunky brown beans. The last time he'd fed her beans, she nearly vomited at the taste. Exactly half her meals felt this way. Normal food, but it was off, feeling gritty and soured or extra spicy and gooey, though not in a hot sense, more like smelling certain kinds of solvents heavy in baking soda and the taste they evoked.

"Mommy, Mommy. Come get me, Mommy."

She continued rocking, her knees pulled tight to her chest. Her gaze was pinned to her breakfast plate, and more specifically, the steel fork half submerged in those nasty beans. He had promised that once she got pregnant, the food would be much better, but until then, it was a waste to give her anything worth eating. It was during this conversation that she realized she recognized his voice more than vaguely. She still hadn't placed it, but it was someone she knew.

Using the word 'pregnant' sparked a memory in an all too honest way. The Dollmaker took girls, held them, and, thanks to the stories of Charlaine Chabot's body, impregnated them if he could. He'd keep a piece of her and discard the rest, no matter what he said. She was dead.

She was dead.

She was dead.

"I'm sorry, Mommy, I'm already dead," she whispered and crawled to the door.

She took the plate, scooped the beans into her waste bucket—after taking a couple disgusting but necessary mouthfuls. She licked the forked clean, then drank deeply from the jug of water the Dollmaker filled once a day. Feet crossed at the ankles, she fell gracefully to the cement floor. The fork would have to do the job.

For six months a few years back, her mother had been fairly serious about a man named Chuck Quick. Chuck was big into hunting and fishing, but mostly into knives. 'Any steel could be a knife if you know what you're doing,' he told her as they stood next to his workbench. He'd never let Melissa touch any of the knives he made, not when he first crafted them. Once they dulled some, sure. Despite this, she watched the man, watched the angle of the steel against the grinder. Other times, she watched him work a whetstone against blades, all without knowing she was gathering anything of use.

She didn't think she'd overpower the Dollmaker, not even if she stabbed or sliced him with a handful of forks. But, if she sharpened her fork into a blade, she could open her wrists without undue pain and fuck up this prick's plan. So, she worked the fork against the cement floor, slowly, almost expertly. It would take time, but time she had.

She figured.

36

Nick and Jaqi had spoken to Pierre after pooling their knowledge and coming to a decidedly suggestive conclusion. What he said had them both aching to get away from the apartment and get busy. They weren't cops, they didn't have weapons or backup, they didn't have training in takedowns. Both Nick and Jaqi had begun to argue, but Pierre promised this wasn't about giving the case to the cops—they'd almost certainly ignore it since charges had been pressed against Mikey Keane—it was about making sure they didn't get themselves killed.

He would go talk to Kris Edler himself, then he'd speak to Kris' known friends. If the man ran, they had him. If he didn't, and nothing with the friends panned out, then perhaps they'd followed a trail of pyrite rather than gold.

It had been late into the evening by the time they'd gotten hold of Pierre, and he promised to go around first thing, then to their apartment before noon.

Eleven o'clock came and went.

Twelve o'clock came and went.

One o'clock came and went.

At 1:49 PM, their phone rang, and Jaqi sprinted from the evidence wall to the kitchen.

"Hello?"

"Is this Jaqi Bazinet?" The voice was feminine, raspy, and curt.

"Yes?"

"My name's Alexis Schwabe; I'm a nurse down at Guelph General. Pierre Allard awoke this afternoon after last night's surgery—"

"Surgery!"

"Please, don't interrupt me. Yes, surgery. He was airlifted from the Delson Hospital last night. He's stable and asked me to tell you he was sorry, but he hadn't been able to talk to anyone."

"He… Is he going to be okay?"

"He'll survive, but it will be an adjustment learning to live with one arm."

"One arm!" Jaqi looked at Nick with eyes like high beams on a moonless night.

"Yes, but now I have to go. Please, don't come. He won't be able to see anyone for at least a few days."

"Okay, I—" The line disconnected in Jaqi's ear. She hung up. "There was a car accident. Pierre was flown down to Guelph General."

"Fuck off," Nick said, disbelief thick in the words.

Jaqi sighed. "Do we wait…I don't want to wait. I mean, what if it's him?"

Nick made a pained expression. "Guess maybe we should call the cops and see what they say about it."

The surprise, the letdown, the worry fled her face on a sneer. "No. Pierre said Kris Edler has four or five close friends. We find out where they live and we visit them.

It'll likely be safe if we don't actually go to Kris himself."

"I doubt townhall will be open, that's where they keep property information."

Jaqi yanked open the door of a side table they'd acquired from a used furniture store called Twice Loved. She scooped the fat phone book and slammed it down on the coffee table, emphasizing the great resource they had right there.

"We have, what, four names? And one of them is in holding still, right?"

Nick sighed. "Right. Right."

They sat on the couch, the phonebook open on the coffee table. There were no Orlovs in the book, so they didn't know where to find the man called Andrei. Zach Soderberg was automatically off the list, but they noted his address anyway. The third name was Pete Maciver; Piere had said he wasn't local, though they checked just in case. The fourth name was Colin Labanc. There were two C. Labancs listed: one in town and one out of town.

"I need to get gas, if I'm going out of town," Jaqi said.

"That's fine, I'll go out of town. Just…be careful. Kris Edler might be visiting or on the phone, or maybe tipped this Colin guy off that we were snooping around."

"You really think it's the electrician, even after the way the guy said it to me?" Jaqi said.

Nick put his hands up, as if explaining the whopper of a fish he'd caught. "I feel it. It has to be. We just need to find where he's holding the girls; his house isn't big enough, unless the basement's mammoth, and the garage is just a garage."

"So, whichever one of us finds this Colin guy, we ask soft questions, then get around to his friends, then ask if Kris has land somewhere?"

Nick let his arms drop as Jaqi spoke. "Sounds hopeless, strung together like that."

37

The clock in her car's stereo read 2:29 PM as Jaqi pulled into Colin Labanc's driveway. The house was quiet, no vehicles were visible, though a tell-tale oil stain suggested where she could've expected to see a vehicle. She backed out, and as she waited for an old man to putt by on a riding lawnmower, two ideas struck: she'd ask at the town's only full-service, accredited beautician, then check the bus station, he was a driver after all…after she filled her tank.

―

It took four minutes to get to the gravel road listed in the phonebook. The green signs at the ends of the long laneways jumped at strange intervals and Nick found himself questioning his location every time he saw a new number.

"At least they're going in the right direction, still," he said to himself, the numbers shrinking with each sign.

He crawled his car along the road, stopping every half-mile or so to read another property sign. Then, there it was. The lane went on and on, a barn and a shed, both formally red but now looking a sun-bleached maroon. He parked about twenty feet from the barn. Two things became immediately obvious: nobody lived here and someone visited often. The grass was mowed, sloppily, but mowed, though maybe hadn't been in a few weeks.

Nick went to the barn's open front and looked inside. It was empty but for the remnants of past farm activity: strands of straw and hay, a faded and rusty pitchfork leaning against a wall, and a wooden pulley system dropping a few feet from the high, high ceiling.

"Anybody here?" he said.

Nick lit a cigarette and continued to look around; he'd come all the way out here, after all. The shed was closed up. He peered through the man-door's windows. Inside were an ancient Massey-Fergusson tractor in red and grease, rusty in the wheels, and a green and red round baler, paled almost to grey. There was a workbench littered with rusty tools, filthy jugs, bits of twine, and three dead pigeons. He leaned tight, trying to see deeper to his left. He spotted two snowmobiles, one recent, one ancient. The ancient one was a John Deere.

"Didn't know they made snowmobiles," he said.

He put his hand on the door handle but decided breaking and entering was not a suitable meal for today's menu. He cupped his hands once more and scanned the shed's interior for *something*.

—

Melissa was a mess of tears and swipes of blood that rose up from her wrists. So far, the most she could bring herself to do was to scratch. It made her cry harder. It was as if those tears gored her innards away like an augur through ice, displacing what held her shape, leaving behind only a puddle.

She took six deep breaths, then screamed, pressed the sharpened fork to her wrist, and as it had every time before, a little voice whispered in her mind, *what if someone comes*. Shaking, trying to force the steel deep, she folded back, splaying herself on the cool concrete, hardly human anymore. Just a puddle of skin and bones.

—

"I don't know. I used to sell Mary Kay; you know. That was way back."

Jaqi smiled, encouraging the woman at the salon to continue. Jaqi had gotten lucky, there had been a cancellation, just enough time to get her hair tidied and ask some questions.

"Before you became a beautician?" Jaqi said, eyes closed as the woman trim the tips from her bangs.

"Yep. I wasn't bad, but the lady who trained me had a monopoly; well, almost."

"Ah, I've heard it's territorial," Jaqi said, trying to ignore a snip of hair that had found her tongue.

"Maryanne was amazing. She'd get money out of people who didn't have money to spend. Mary Kay gave her a car once, she sold so much. That's a big deal; Mary

Kay is a bit of a pyramid scheme, but like an okay one. I mean, the cosmetics and nail polish are very good. Shame this killer's giving the stuff a bad name."

"Maryanne?" Jaqi said, recalling that this Maryanne had been mentioned before. "That's Maryanne Lebeau, correct?"

"Labanc."

Jaqi frowned. "Labanc? Would she be related to Colin?"

"Well, she's dead. But that's her son, yes."

The math was coming together. Jaqi had to remind herself to breathe. No way Kris Edler couldn't have gotten old cosmetics from his buddy Colin. Jesus. She could hardly wait to hear what Nick discovered.

After paying, Jaqi thanked the woman and headed back out to Colin Labanc's home. When he wasn't there, she drove to Petre-Canada to fill her tank. She wished Nick had a bag phone; they suddenly felt closer than close.

Tank full, Jaqi rolled into the bus depot lot. It was a huge space and was currently all but empty aside from drivers' personal vehicles and a few buses parked near the roll up doors of a large, multi-bay shop. There was a mechanic in blue coveralls leaned over the engine compartment of a city bus. Surely, this guy would know if Colin Labanc was working.

"Hello?"

The man slunk himself out, 10mm wrench in one hand, a bolt in the other. "Yeah?"

"Do you know if Colin Labanc is working?"

The man looked around the lot. "That's his car, so I guess he is."

"Do you know where I could find him?"

The mechanic tipped his head down, inadvertently showing off the bald patch at the top-rear of his cranium. "Think…think he does four routes: Seven-A, Four-B, Six-B, and One-C."

Jaqi looked at the man with uplifted brows.

He got it immediately. "Of course, why would some random girl know where those are, even a pretty girl like you."

Jaqi wondered, briefly, what in the hell her looks could possibly have to do with her knowing or not knowing the bus routes. Her brain instantly filled in that it had to do with everything where this man was concerned. Whether she was pretty or not was the *only* thing that mattered with a man like this.

"Over by the main door there," the mechanic pointed, "there's a plastic thing on the wall. Has all the routes mapped out."

"Seven-A, Four-B, Seven-B, and One-C?"

"Yeah. No. Seven-A, Four-B, Six-B, and One-C."

Jaqi offered a small smile. "Thank you." She turned and started away, smile gone before she'd gone an entire step.

"You know, I could let you drive a bus, feel that big power," the mechanic called after her.

Jaqi hardly heard it; waitressing had made her all but

immune to men, and when they got beneath her skin, they got stabbed. She took the pamphlet and unfolded it as she stepped back to her car. Before she could forget, she scribbled the routes on an empty space as she sat behind the wheel, key hanging uselessly in the ignition.

"Seven-A," she said and started toward Wellington Street.

—

Nick turned from his car—he'd been ready to leave—at the sound of a vehicle barreling up the laneway. As the driver parked, dust billowed but dropped quickly, and Nick held up a hand as if miming *stop*. The man climbed out. He wore a concerned expression and Nick decided he'd better talk quickly.

"Hey, are you Colin?"

The man closed the driver's door. He had a square head and broad shoulders, arms ropey with wiry muscle. He wore a bus driver's uniform.

"Who's asking?"

Nick held out a hand. "I'm Nick Price. I'm working on a story about the social impact of a serial killer on a small town."

"Why, you think they didn't catch the guy? They have a couple guys in custody."

"Think they only charged one."

"Right."

Nick grinned. "My story is about the people, not the Dollmaker."

Colin nodded slowly. "I thought it was a woman

looking for me?"

"I don't know about that. Might've been—"

A scream carried on the gentle breeze, coming from a patch of tamped down grass far across the yard. Nick looked that way. It was a girl, that sound was a girl screaming.

"If you can be quiet, I'll let you in on a secret," Colin said, eyes blazing, sweat pebbling his forehead.

"Secret?"

"Not my secret," Colin said, turning and waving over his shoulder and stage whispering, "It's a fox den and the mother just had kits. They sound just like little kids. It's why I came out. This is my folks' place; they've passed."

Nick followed, glancing into the front seat of Colin's Ford Ranger as he went by. There was a duffle bag on the seat with a yawning zipper. Inside, he saw a box with the word Kay emblazoned along the top. He kept walking.

The screaming grew louder and louder as they drew closer, though was still greatly muffled. He hardly heard it, trying to remember why he knew the name Kay. When it finally hit him, he was standing ten feet away from a submarine style bulkhead, door and wheel handle painted green and sunk into the lawn.

Kay, Mary Kay, a makeup brand women sold door-to-door.

Makeup.

Colin turned around, his face relaxed, almost drooping. "I've never had to kill a man," he said, then closed the distance between them in a flash.

Nick had never been in a fight. His arms came up uselessly. The first punch slammed a black blotch over his vision that lingered two seconds before reverse burning, giving Nick a good view of Colin's second punch. His knees went out and he crumpled to the scratchy lawn, barely clinging to consciousness.

—

The map stretched strangely in the pamphlet, but Jaqi found Seven-A. It was a familiar area. She pulled up to a streetlight behind a Bronco with black smoke puffing from its tailpipe. If she hooked a right—a handful of feet past a bus stop—she'd have to drive maybe thirty seconds to reach Elise Tabaracci's home.

The light went green, and she rolled on. At the next stoplight—and next bus stop—she could hook a left and reach Pheobe Huddy's home inside a minute. When the light turned, her foot remained firm on the brake pedal. She had the map open over her steering wheel. Behind her, a horn blasted. She heard nothing but an intense ringing, her mind superimposing the map from her living room wall over the bus routes. Nearly all the kidnapping occurred less than a block from a bus stop.

What if Kris Edler lent his uniform to a man with a stockpile of cosmetics?

"Nick," she whispered, then slammed the gas pedal.

38

Melissa panted shallow breaths, attempting to psych herself into action. Distantly, she heard the closing of a door—she had no way of knowing it was more of a hatch. She heard nothing more and resumed carving her flesh, her mind screaming, *What if! What if! What if someone comes for you!*

The sharpened fork pressed into a deep scratch, following its groove, blood bubbling but hardly flowing. She screamed again, willing herself to do it, do it, do it!

—

Jaqi pulled over at the first payphone she saw. It was old enough that emergency numbers were listed on a faded strip of paper above the receiver.

She punched the three digits, heard a single ring before a feminine voice said, "What's your emergency?"

Jaqi took a deep breath. "Melissa Sparks is being held at a farm outside town. The killer, the real one, is a man named Colin Labanc. He uses Kris Edler's police uniform to—"

"Ma'am, what's your name?" the dispatcher said, sounding far from amused.

"Jaqi Bazinet."

"You know it's a misdemeanor crime to occupy emergency lines unnecessarily?"

"Shut the fuck up, you stupid bitch and listen! Send someone to Colin Labanc's farm!"

The dispatcher clicked her tongue. "I'm going to hang up now." It was almost possible to hear her resume filing down her nails.

"No! Listen!"

"You're committing a crime."

When Jaqi heard that dead line's pulse, she screamed, began smashing the receiver against the telephone's rugged body. After a dozen or so strikes, she broke for her still running car. She had the address in her notes; she had to get there, she had to get there fast.

—

Nick was more out than in, but he was coming to. He felt himself flop and bounce, then fall flat on a hard surface. He peered through one squinted eye. Directly above him was a ladder and the underside of the hatch he'd seen earlier. The only scent coming to him was the smell of blood. He attempted to roll over, but Colin's big black boots were inches from his face.

Colin bent and grabbed Nick by the left wrist. The pain was instantaneous, though nothing Nick couldn't stay quiet through as Colin dragged him over the smooth cement floor. The screaming was clear now, as was his mistake.

Colin lifted Nick onto a sturdy wooden dining chair. Before Nick's mind could sum the ingredients of what was happening, he was zip-tied to the chair, arms and legs. After a few moderate slaps, Colin struck Nick hard enough that he could no longer feign unconsciousness.

"There you are. How did you figure me out?"

Nick's lips felt huge. The taste of blood was heavy in his mouth. He mumbled, "Thought it was Edler."

Colin straightened. "Kris Edler? Why?"

"Old uniform...moustache...witnesses seeing a cop they couldn't recognize." Nick was fully awake now, and terrified, but he was playing a dope, trying to think of something, anything. He blinked as his head lolled, looking around the room. In a far corner was a deeply mummified corpse sitting in a recliner, face plastered in makeup, hair done up fresh for 1983. Above the corpse was an 8x10 in a cheap gold frame. It was Colin with a woman about twenty-five years his senior.

"Not bad. Bet you feel almost smart."

"No," Nick said after a pause.

"Now, who's the chick looking for me?"

Nick shook his head in rough, jerky strokes. "No," he said. "No."

Colin sighed. He turned from Nick and headed for the part of the bunker obviously dedicated to cooking. When he started back, he had a filleting knife in hand.

Colin pressed the knife to Nick's head. "Who is she?"

"I don't—ah!" Nick howled as the knife slipped between his right ear and his face, lobbing the cartilage and flesh free in a sickly sluice that sounded like a bullhorn in Nick's now unprotected ear hole. "Stop! No!"

"Her name?" Colin said again.

Nick tried to jerk a hand free; anything to protect himself. "Josie...Josie Wells."

Colin tutted. "The girl's name is Josie Wells, like the

outlaw?"

"Yes!"

"Liar!"

Colin stabbed at Nick's face, the blade slipping into his right eyeball, sending a flash of pain and light into his head before he slipped into dark agony.

"Please," Nick mumbled, blood and saliva oozing from his puffy lips as his deflated eye wept ocular fluid.

"Don't want to talk? I've got an idea.

Jaqi found the driveway and gunned it halfway up the lane, her foot pressing the gas pedal deeper when she saw Nick's car and, assumedly, Colin Labanc's truck. She parked and kicked open her door as she spun back the key. She filled her lungs to shout but stopped short.

Screaming, she heard screaming.

It was muffled, but undeniably a human, female. Her panicked eyes scanned the yard. The weeds and grass were out of control everywhere but in a single section; she hurried that way, not knowing what to look for. The screams were slightly louder. She walked, looking at the tall grass, expecting to see an opening of some fashion, which was when she tripped and went sprawling sideways. When she looked back, she saw the hatch. Crawling, she grabbed hold of the wheel, but didn't spin, didn't pull.

First, she needed something from her car.

―

The door opened and Melissa stuffed the sharpened fork

into the waistband of her pajama pants. "The bus driver?" she said, seeing her captor's face for the first time.

"Stupid cunt. Look at the mess you've made," Colin said, charging forward and taking a handful of hair. He began to drag her.

Melissa held onto her pants, feeling the fork slip down into a leg. Colin didn't drag her far, leaving her like a moist heap on the floor before a bloodied man. As nonchalantly as possible, she snaked a hand down the back of her pants, but stopped dead when she felt the knife's tip slip into her ear, itching to slam through, into her brain.

Death no longer seemed a good option.

"Tell me her name or this bitch gets it," Colin said, looking at Nick.

Nick, nearly out of it, oozing all over, spat, then said, "Jaqi Bazinet. Please, don't hurt me anymore."

"Address?"

Nick gave it without a second's hesitation.

"Thank you," Colin said, pulling the knife away from Melissa and pressing it sideways into Nick's chest, an inch from his breastbone and through his heart. When he pulled the blade free, the pressure was great enough to spurt three quick pumps, all nailing Melissa on the cheek.

She screamed again.

"Will you shut up!" Nick shouted, cocking the knife back behind his right ear, poised to slash, Anthony Perkins style.

—

Just as Jaqi grabbed the hatch, another scream let loose, covering the gentle creak of the hidden hinges. She popped her head down, seeing Nick, seeing Melissa Sparks, and seeing Colin Labanc. All three were bloody, but only Nick was drenched, only Nick was slumped.

She put the steak knife she'd accidentally stolen from the golf course between her teeth like she was on the verge of some swashbuckling. She started down the short ladder—the ceiling of the bunker was no more than seven feet from the floor.

Colin stopped mid-slash and said, "Let me guess, Jaqi Bazinet!" His tone was amused and exhilarated.

Jaqi jumped, losing her footing and falling the final four rungs to the floor. Colin swung a lazy, sideways slash, forcing her back down when she attempted to rise. He swung again, a little more intensely this time.

"How fucking dare you invade my mother's space." He slashed again.

Jaqi was squirming away when the knife cut a gulley into her forearm. She let out a scream and Colin laughed. She felt the steak knife beneath her and rolled far enough to get it in her hand. She brought it up and the excitement on Colin's face evaporated.

"All right. No playing around then."

He reared back and followed through, booting her in the chest in a way that sucked all the air from her lungs and left her a gasping heap on the floor. He cocked back, again poised to slash downward.

He did not kill her.

His eyes went wide, wide, wide and his knees shook a moment before he tumbled, as if the power on his battery had drained. Melissa climbed over him, forcing the fork in his spine a little deeper. She grabbed his knife, fixing a two-hand grip. Blood was oozing slowly from her left wrist. Colin moaned, working his jaw around, his eyes bouncing erratically like super balls.

"You fuck!" Melissa growled as she slammed the knife into Colin's groin from behind. She pulled the blade free, and did it again, and again. She only stopped when Jaqi gently touched her shoulder.

39

Jaqi had to do a photo-op for her forthcoming book: *Integrity Against the Willfully Blind: the True Story of the Delson Dollmaker.* It had been eight months since she'd climbed out of that bunker. She hadn't gone back to school, though she had moved back to London. Delson was not a happy place for her.

Robert, Rube, Rube the Tractor Tube, Thompson had retired from his post as chief, and no new chief had been named as rumblings of letting the OPP take over things in town grew louder and louder. That didn't mean much.

Pierre Allard had to retire from the badge, resuming a

much more natural fit as an attorney. Jaqi saw him now, waiting by the prison gates, one sleeve of his suit jacket pinned about four inches above his elbow, and broke into a jog.

She grabbed him from behind and said, "Guess who."

"Umm, Santa Claus?" Pierre said, glancing over his shoulder.

Before she could say more, a heavy door clanked open and an old man stepped out. He was wispy bald with a doughy build and moist eyes. It was clear, even from a distance, that he hadn't been dealt a full hand of cards. He waddled toward the last fence between incarceration and freedom. Jaqi let go of Pierre and came to stand next to him. Behind them, reporters snapped shots and called names, but were wholly ignored. A guard opened the fence gate and the man stepped out, fourteen years older than when he went in.

"Mr. Allard!"

"Donny Tiffany, the free man." Pierre took Donny by the hand and pulled him in for a one-armed hug. "Donny, there's someone I want you to meet."

"Ms. Bazinet?" Donny said.

Pierre nudged her with his elbow. "That's right. The reason you're free. A true hero."

Jaqi blushed. "It's very nice to meet you, Donny."

"Thank you for not thinking I kill girls," Donny said, smile huge, revealing teeth so yellow they almost glowed. Jaqi rubbed his shoulder, feeling the rough fabric of the now too small Carhart jacket he'd entered wearing.

"Guess we'd better get the shots," she said, and turned to face the cameras. She stood on Donny's left and Pierre stood on his right. The eight reporters holding cameras snapped dozens of shots, while those with video cameras simply let the film roll.

—

"I was so sad for you when I heard about Nick," Pierre said.

They'd escaped the crowds and found a quiet café with booths to settle down and catch up. Both had simple cups of coffee before them.

"Yes, it's been difficult. I kind of assumed we'd get married someday," Jaqi said. "How's rehab gone?"

Pierre motor-boated his lips through a sigh. "I can still feel my arm. And the things I said to my physiotherapist when he was pushing me…I dare not repeat in public. But I'm alive and well, and that's enough for now."

"I suppose."

A weighty silence settled between them that stretched on for more than a minute.

"So, you've dropped out?" Pierre said.

"Just for now, but I'm going to switch majors. My dad's not impressed, but he doesn't have to pay for me anymore, so it doesn't really matter what he thinks."

Pierre put his hand up like a mime finding and invisible wall. "Don't say if you don't want, but how much was the advance?"

Jaqi leaned in and whispered, "Just under five hundred."

"Five hundred thousand?" Pierre shouted, then looked around. The waitress was looking at them, as was an old woman gumming her dentures around her rubbery mouth. "You could work part time for the rest of your life, if you're smart."

"I'm going to start on another book. In fact, at the end of the month I'm giving back my keys and moving out to Saskatchewan to investigate a town where nine women have disappeared in the last three years. South Peaceford. Have you heard of it?"

Pierre shook his head.

"It's a boomtown, but it's been around since the turn of the century."

A strange expression slipped onto Pierre's face. He took his remaining hand from his mug and put it over Jaqi's right hand. "You know, I think you're going to change the world, and whatever it costs you personally, we'll all benefit from your existence."

Too choked up to speak, Jaqi freed her hand and lifted her mug high. "A toast, to Nick Price."

"To Nick Price," Pierre said, and drank deeply.

ATLAS WUNDOR

SUMMERY OF FINDINGS FROM WITHIN THE LABANC BUNKER

Stockpile of Mary Kay Cosmetics and nail polish
Breast pump
Disposable underwear in three adult sizes
Glass cutting tools
One police uniform, including badge and sidearm
Three professional grade human hair moustaches
Food and water, both recently purchased and decades old
Four small rooms with cots
One case of pregnancy tests
Two cells built into the walls separating the small rooms
Mummified human remains: Maryanne Labanc (1926-1982 *estimated)
Mummified human remains: Jessica Labanc (1960-1991 *estimated)
Mummified human remains: Doreen Barber (1968-1986 *estimated)
Mummified human remains: babies x 4: genetic matches to Doreen Barber and Colin Labanc (1984, 1985, 1985, 1986 *estimated)
Trace evidence confirming 39 distinct DNA suppliers